Wrong Side of Hell

Also by Juliana Stone

His Darkest Salvation
His Darkest Embrace
His Darkest Hunger

Wrong Side of Hell

A LEAGUE OF GUARDIANS NOVELLA

JULIANA STONE

AVONIMPULSE

Excerpt from *Wicked Road to Hell* copyright © 2012 by Juliana Stone

EPub Edition MARCH 2012 ISBN: 9780062108104

Print Edition ISBN: 9780062136275

10 9 8 7 6 5 4 3 2 1

Wrong Side of Hell

In the beginning . . .

FOR MILLENNIA THE struggle between light and dark, between the upper and lower realms, has been policed by a secret group of warriors culled from every fabric of existence. They are both otherworld and human, male and female. They are known to each other as the League of Guardians. Their pledge, to protect the line between dominions and make sure neither side grows too powerful. If they should fall, so shall the earth, the heavens, and hells. And there will be no more.

Chapter One

THE DOOR BEHIND Logan Winters opened, bringing with it a gust of wind, the faint scent of pine, and complete silence. Like a ripple effect, conversations stopped, laughter faded, and eyes were averted.

Logan glanced up at the bartender, took notice of the stubby fingers grasped tight to the bottle of Canadian whiskey—the bottle Logan had been waiting for—and scowled.

The Neon Angel was a sad excuse for a drinking hole. It had seen better days, and from what he could tell, so had most of the staff and clientele. The bar was a rickety shack on the edge of a town he had no name for. It was the place he'd ended up—no reason other than timing—and for a brief moment it had been the heaven he'd been seeking.

His eyebrows knit together and his lips tightened. All he'd wanted was a drink. *Just one fucking drink.*

He exhaled and shifted slightly, giving himself more room as he pushed his bar stool back a few inches. The couple that had been sitting to his left were already on their feet, a wad of cash thrown onto the bar as they slid into the shadows that wrapped around the room.

The redhead who'd been eyeing him but good downed her wine and smiled a crazy "I'm getting the hell out of here" kind of smile before wiping the corner of her mouth and turning away.

Guess he wasn't getting laid either.

Logan swore—a harsh string of words no one would understand—and nodded to the bartender. "I'll take that shot now."

The large man ran his free hand through the thinning gray pallet atop his head and swallowed hard, his watery eyes wide as he glanced toward Logan. Thick bands of wiry gray brows curled crazily above round eyeballs the color of peat moss.

He wore a faded black wifebeater t-shirt and his soft arms were filled with tattoos that jiggled as he rubbed the scruff on his chin. "Dude . . . not sure if that would be a good . . . uh . . . idea."

Logan's ice blue eyes narrowed as a snarl caught in the back of his throat. He felt the heat beneath his skin. The burn. The itch.

"Do not," he bared his teeth, "call me dude."

A rumble rose from his chest—a menacing warning— and the bartender took heed, his body jerking in small, quick movements as he stepped forward. Logan nodded toward the bottle, his low rasp barely containing the irritation he felt. "Pour me the drink." He'd have his whiskey and then deal with whoever the hell had decided tonight was a good night to fuck with him.

The bartender swallowed nervously, his Adam's apple bobbing through the thick folds of skin at his neck. He didn't know what to do. Run from whoever—or whatever—had blown into the place or pour the damn whiskey and be done with it.

His eyes darted to just behind Logan once more but he jumped when Logan barked. *"Now."*

The bartender poured a generous amount of whiskey into the tumbler, and though he tried to be careful, his hands shook so much it was a damn miracle he didn't spill the precious liquid all over the place.

The sound of clinking glass echoed into the dead silence, and when the bartender was done, he set the bottle to the side and stepped back. A pronounced tick pulsed near his left eye and he swallowed nervously as he stood there, shuffling his feet, eyes shifting from Logan to the door. His face was flushed a ruddy pink color, the skin shiny with sweat and fear.

Logan tossed some cash onto the dark grained bar and stood, his six-foot-six frame unfurling with the uncanny grace of an animal, which, considering his origins, wasn't surprising.

Tension settled along his wide shoulders as he reached for the glass, but along with it, a shot of anticipation. He was itching for a fight. He'd just not known it until now.

He tipped his head back. Amber liquid slid onto his tongue and he welcomed the smooth, sweet taste. It burned—all the way down—yet he closed his eyes and savored the sensation.

Logan had been pretty much everywhere—in the human realm and beyond—and he could say with certainty Canadians knew how to brew their damn whiskey better than anyone else.

He let the liquid fire settle in his belly, then carefully set the empty glass back onto the bar. He arched a brow and nodded, a slight jerk to the right.

Now would be a good time for the bartender to leave.

Sweat beaded along the man's top lip. It was quickly wiped away by a thick meaty hand, and then the bartender took a step back before he too disappeared into the shadows.

Logan slowly turned.

Two men stood just inside the door of the Neon Angel, their tall frames bathed in shadow. They were big. Well built and muscled.

And they'd not come to socialize.

Logan had no idea who they were, but judging from the otherworld scent that clung to them, he had a pretty good idea where they'd come from. But that was the tricky part, wasn't it? Which realm did they call home?

No scent of demon twisted in the air, and yet . . .

His hands fisted at his sides. He could take them. Hell, he *wanted* to take them.

"Shit, that didn't take you boys long." Logan nodded toward the now empty bar. "You cleared the room in less time than it takes for a junkie with a needle in his vein to get high."

Nothing. There was no expression or words.

Logan remained silent for a few moments and cocked his head to the side. He studied the two creatures—and creatures they were; there was not one drop of humanity in them. His nostrils flared as the subtle scent of pine drifted toward him once more, and he frowned.

A memory stirred, and with it a flush of heat, a dirge of anger.

Slowly his fists unfurled to hang loose at his sides, and Logan leaned back against the bar, elbows resting against the edge, long legs crossed in front of him.

"I'm not much for one-sided conversation, so unless you've got something to say, I'd suggest you turn your asses around and leave." Logan grabbed the bottle of whiskey off the counter. "Cause I've got some drinking to do and that sure as hell *is* something I prefer to do alone."

A low keening vibration rippled through the room—an invisible thread that electrified the air and sent his radar crashing into full-on red alert.

Bright light lit the men from behind, beams so intense Logan took a step back and winced. His skin burned as if it had been touched by flames, and the control he had was fast slipping away.

Stars danced in front of his eyes and he shook his head aggressively as he moved forward, his mind emptying of all thoughts except one. Survival.

There was power here. Old, ancient power—the kind that always signaled shit was about to hit. *Hard*. Logan was determined that any ass kicking in the immediate future would not involve his own.

Sifting beams of light sizzled and popped, and for a second he saw nothing but glitter, small pulsating fragments of gold that drifted on the breeze and whirled around the shadowed forms. They merged, twirling faster as the keening vibrations became louder and they melted together into one large vortex of light.

Logan glared straight ahead, his gut tightening as the pine scent that hung in the air sharpened. It was fresh, tangy . . . and all too familiar.

His anger spiked as one form emerged from what had been two: a smallish, round bit of a man who looked nothing like what he truly was—Seraphim—and he was one of the original seven. Humans might call him angel, though in this form he bore no resemblance to the golden creatures popular in lore.

This was no fucking cherub.

"Askelon," Logan said smoothly, his anger in check, his façade calm.

"Let's not be so formal, my friend."

Glittery gold lamé lapels glistened against his gray jacket as the small man moved forward. His pants were ill fitting, a little too snug around his generous belly, and his dress shirt sported gaping holes between the buttons. Something was smeared alongside his mouth—ketchup? And in his hand he held a bag of—Logan sniffed—candy.

Good to see his sweet tooth was still intact. "A little theatrical, even for you, don't you think?"

Askelon arched a brow and shrugged his shoulders.

"Your bodyguards?" Logan continued dryly.

The small man laughed. "Ah . . . that was nothing. Parlor tricks, really. I somehow doubt this room would have emptied if I stood as myself, and I do so want a private chat. We've lots to discuss."

Logan's eyes narrowed as he watched him walk to the bar, throw his bag of candy—which Logan could now see was filled to the brim with colorful little bits of sugar—and with a little effort, settle himself onto the bar stool Logan had just vacated.

"Gummies."

"What?" He frowned, a scowl sweeping across his face as he stared at the little man.

Askelon nodded toward the bag. "They're called Gummi Bears."

Arms crossed, Logan's scowl deepened. "I hope you have one hell of a dental plan. That shit will rot your teeth out."

Askelon's pudgy fingers grasped a napkin and wiped away the stains on his face as he turned to Logan. For a second his eyes shimmered—a weird translucent silver color—and Logan saw the power that shifted within their depths.

"Please," he smiled and nodded, "call me Bill."

"Bill?" Logan's eyebrow arched in disbelief.

Bill grinned, shrugged, and proceeded to pour himself a glass of whiskey. "It's plain, I know, but suited me at the time." He poured one for Logan and handed it to him, raising his own in a toast.

What the hell do you want with me?

"I'll explain in a minute but first, let's drink, shall we? That is why you came here tonight, isn't it? To drink? Perhaps forget?"

So he was a mind reader now.

The tension that had fled moments earlier was back, pinching his shoulders as Logan reached for the glass and tossed back the tumbler full of booze.

The little round shit was responsible for his banishment as surely as if he'd . . .

"You know that's not true, Logan."

Logan's chest heaved. He gritted his teeth and slammed the glass back onto the counter.

"Stay the fuck out of my head, Seraphim." Logan moved forward until he was close enough to see the veins in the little shit's eyes. His nostrils flared and his chest grumbled. Beneath his skin, the beast stirred.

"Your banishment was unfortunate." Bill sipped the whiskey, his eyes shimmering as they regarded Logan closely. "But you knew there would be consequences when you joined the League."

Logan snorted. "Yeah, well. Your so-called League can go screw itself."

Bill set his half-empty glass onto the counter and twirled the liquid slowly with his finger as silence fell between them.

He turned to Logan and though his voice was soft, there was no mistaking the hard glint in his eyes. "That's not how it works, my friend."

Logan snarled and whirled away. He was a hellhound. His job was to retrieve souls that were beyond redemption and escort them to District Three—one of several levels in hell—for processing.

He neither liked nor hated his job, but he sure as hell was the best kind of animal for it. He was an elite hellhound shifter, born from the depths of hell and destined to straddle the realms. His hunting capabilities were legendary, his sensory skills unparalleled.

Logan's lips curled as the faint smell of pine tugged at him once more. He stared at the mirror that hung on the wall in front of him. At a reflection so bizarre it was laughable. Askelon had outdone himself. His human façade was nothing short of brilliant. No one would ever suspect the short, round, balding man was in fact one of the most powerful beings in existence. If not *the* most.

Anger spiraled through him and Logan took a step toward *Bill*, not caring that the ancient could dish out a hell of a lot of damage with nothing more than the flick of his wrist.

He growled and passed his hands through the thick hair at his nape.

"Why are you here?" The last time he'd seen the little fuck, Logan's life had taken a header right into the fires of hell. Literally. He'd defied direct orders from his Overlord because Bill had asked him to. Logan had led a child back into the human realm—one he'd been ordered to retrieve for processing—and he'd been brutally punished.

He'd been sentenced to the Pit—*the* shit hole many leagues beneath District Three. It was the one place in hell that everyone avoided, if they were smart or had occasion to. It was saying something that he, a creature born of fire and brimstone, had nearly been broken by it.

"I need your help, Logan."

Logan paused, his face incredulous. "What part of 'shove your fucking League of Guardians up your ass' didn't you understand the last time?" He arched a brow and smiled, his lips tight in a sarcastic grin. "Or is this something else entirely? You pulling a Vader and crossing over to the dark side, Bill?" He flexed his arms—let his beast shift beneath the surface. "You want a ride down? Is that it?"

"The girl has been killed."

"What girl?" A frown crossed Logan's face. He didn't like where the conversation was headed, and he really didn't like the direction his mind was going.

"The same girl you were ordered to drag below fifteen years ago." Bill sighed, rubbed his temples. "The one we saved." If Logan didn't know better, he'd think the little shit was tired.

"We? Seems to me, I did all the work and had my ass kicked for hundreds of years because of it." Logan shook his head. No way was he getting involved again. "I'm done. I don't give a flying fuck about that girl." Did the Seraphim think he cared if she was dead? As far as Logan was concerned, she'd been on borrowed time anyway. If anything, she'd been granted a reprieve while he'd rotted beneath District Three.

Time moved differently there. In the Pit. What had been fifteen years to the human girl had been nearly fifteen hundred for Logan.

"Tsk, tsk . . . language, my friend." Bill turned fully

and nailed Logan with a direct stare. "You should care. We all need to care."

"You're talking in circles, old man. Elaborate or leave."

Bill's mouth tightened for the briefest moment and Logan knew he'd overstepped with his last statement. He smiled, liking the fact that he managed to get under Askelon's skin. Score one for the hound.

"She cannot perish. Her future is hidden in the fabric that binds us all. But know this." Bill's nostrils flared as his anger thickened. "She will be protected. I will do everything in my power to keep her safe and make sure she meets her destiny."

"Seems like a moot point, considering she's already dead."

Bill's eyes narrowed. His face darkened and blurred . . . features shifting until his true self shone through. Gone was the pleasant, middle-aged human. In his stead a powerful, enigmatic creature stood. Two realities converged, and Logan had to admit the little shit's mojo was impressive.

Bill's voice vibrated, falling in layers that encircled Logan and filled his head. There was no mistaking. The Seraphim was livid.

"She is not meant to die—not yet. Someone is trying to alter her destiny and I need you to retrieve her for me."

"She's not my problem. Find some other dog."

"Oh, but she is your problem. I need someone who can track her. Someone who knows her scent." Bill leaned closer, his voice amplified even more. "Someone who's tasted her soul."

Logan had had enough. He growled and bared his teeth. "I don't take orders from you. Not anymore. I don't know why I ever agreed to it in the first place."

Bill sighed, grabbed his bag of candy, and helped himself to a generous amount of the gooey mess. "You joined the League because you knew it was the right thing to do. Nothing's changed." He chewed and stared up at Logan, his hard eyes and unyielding mouth at odds with the image he portrayed.

"You will do this for me."

Logan crossed his arms over his chest and spread his legs. The Seraphim was going to have to do a hell of a lot better than that.

Logan reached for the nearly empty bottle of whiskey and dumped the last of it into his glass. "You've wasted a trip, old man." He was dancing on the edge—tossing insults to one of the most powerful creatures in existence—and he didn't give a shit.

Such was the way of it these days. His stay in the Pit had altered him in more ways than one.

"You will do this because of your vow to the League." Bill arched a brow. "And because I know your true origins." The words slid between them—silky, dangerous. Bill's ace in the hole.

Logan paused, the glass nearly to his lips. His throat tightened and his teeth clenched hard.

"I know who your mother is."

The glass shattered in Logan's hand as a snarl erupted from within his chest. In a flash, his fist closed around Bill's throat and he shoved the Seraphim back onto the bar with such force that the walls shook sending bottles and glasses crashing to the floor.

Logan's skin shifted and the beast shone through, his eyes morphing to blood red as he stared down at the small man held tight in his grip.

Several long moments passed and eventually Logan pulled back, curses in an ancient tongue flying from his mouth as he stepped away.

He closed his eyes, forced his body to relax, and crooked his head to the side. "Where's the girl?"

There was a pause.

"Purgatory."

Logan swore. "I don't have permission to enter the gray realm, you know that. No hellhound has ever breached it." He swore again. "And even if I did, there's no guarantee I will get to her in time or find my way out."

"This is true." Bill nodded. "But I have faith in you Logan. I always have."

Logan clenched his lips together tightly and took a few moments to gather his thoughts. He had no choice and he hated that the little son of a bitch had put him in this situation. Hadn't he given enough to the fucking League?

He glared at the Seraphim and spoke coldly. "Where's her body?"

"The Regent Psychiatric Institute in Florida." At Logan's snarl, the round man finished quietly. "Morgue."

The word had barely escaped Bill's lips and Logan was already gone.

Chapter Two

THE REGENT PSYCHIATRIC Institute was a large, rambling estate built at the edge of a hidden inlet deep in the mosquito-infested keys of Florida. At one time it had been home to one of the most notorious pirates in the Caribbean—Banshee McGee—nicknamed such because he kept in his employ a woman who sang the death chant when they were about to attack—and coincidentally, death followed hard in its wake.

A bastard through and through, McGee had plundered the Caribbean for nearly twenty years until he'd met a violent end at a gentlemen's club on Grand Bahama Island. Some thought he'd fittingly been killed by the banshee in his employ, others surmised the devil had finally taken him below.

After his death, the estate had been seized by the government, and eventually the large mansion had been converted into a mental hospital. At one time a special wing had been devoted to the most dangerous of the criminally insane, but late in the nineteenth century it had been sold to a private organization and had been restored to its former grandeur. Now, only those with wads of cash could afford to hide away their crazy family members.

Like Kira Dove. Her family was loaded. This was a detail Logan remembered clearly. When he'd come for her fifteen years ago, she'd been ensconced behind the gilded gates of a mansion in Beverly Hills. Her parents were famous and known the world over. The father was a renowned avant-garde director, and the mother, a model-turned-actress, was his muse.

Logan glanced toward the imposing structure. Kira Dove must have gone buck-crazy to warrant a stay in this place. How long had she been here? That was a question he'd not bothered to ask.

He moved forward and quickly pushed the notion aside. It was none of his concern.

It was easy for Logan to slip past the guards, to blend into the shadows that crept along the edges of the estate. Tall, moss covered trees flanked both sides of the large antebellum home, and in the distance the scent of water drifted on the breeze. Insects buzzed and the occasional hoot of an owl greeted his ears. Other than that, the darkness hid nothing but absolute silence.

Logan strode toward the front entrance, shoulders squared, gait long and loose. His thick wavy hair was slicked back, damp from the humidity, while his dark t-shirt and worn faded jeans blended together to hide him among the shadows.

He paused just inside the front entrance. The lighting here was muted and the dark corners were long. A lamp several feet away in the parlor cast a small pool of light, but it was enough to afford him some illumination.

Palm trees—six feet in height—lined the foyer, their tips waving slowly as large white fans overhead turned in gentle wide arcs. The subtle aroma of a Cuban cigar hung in the air, and he knew someone had passed by recently with one of the golden treasures. His nostrils flared. Montecristo, by the smell of it.

The walls were a delicate yellow with white trim and the floor-to-ceiling windows were open, though the blinds were drawn. Long gossamer curtains rippled on either side like wisps of vanilla smoke. Classic paintings adorned the walls—landscapes and leisurely scenes of the Old South—and small groupings of white wicker furniture were scattered about. Directly ahead was a formal reception area and behind the desk, chewing gum in a loud annoying manner, sat a large woman.

Her hair was a wild mess of tight curls in a harsh shade of red, the kind only a bad perm could produce, and her skin shone like wax paper under the lights. Watery brown eyes peered at him. "Who's there?" she asked in a thin voice.

Logan sensed her alarm as he moved forward, and when he stepped into the light her alarm turned to fear. He moved fast—faster than the human eye—and stood in front of her as she gazed up at him, mouth open, yellowed teeth wet and shiny.

He leaned forward and leveled steely blue eyes onto her. "Morgue."

She swallowed, her eyes glazing over as she nodded, head bobbing like a bouncing ball. "West wing, all the way to the end."

Logan glanced behind her. "Let me in." The compulsion that colored his words was subtle but it was enough. "Speak of this to no one and turn off the cameras."

The woman deactivated the security, and a loud click echoed into the foyer as the heavy steel door retracted into the wall. She resumed smacking her gum, a strange melody falling from her lips as her raspy voice filled the silence.

As soon as Logan cleared the entrance and walked into the facility, the smells changed. No longer was the pleasing odor of tobacco present, or the honeyed scent of flowers. They'd been replaced with fear, pain, and the wildness of chaos. His nostrils flared and he smiled. It was like candy to a creature such as him. Better than any drug imaginable.

Logan strode down the hall, long arms loose at his sides as he turned to his left. Within seconds he spied the door to the morgue. The sterile scent of disinfectant— pine cleaner, to be exact—tickled his nostrils. Bingo.

Time was running out. According to Bill, she'd been dead less than two hours. If Logan was lucky, there would be energy traces left on her body—a signature he'd be able to track with ease. On a normal run—one sanctioned by his Demon Overlord Santos—this was already provided, because the soul had been marked and claimed by the underworld.

This trip, however, was under the radar, and if he had no starting point, he'd be running blind. It would take much longer to find her based on the little bits of her soul he'd tasted all those years ago. He needed something fresh and current. Purgatory wasn't the kind of place a hellhound wanted to linger—it wasn't natural for him to be there—so whatever he could do to hurry along the process would be a good thing.

Besides, there was also a timing issue. Her human form had to be in good shape when he retrieved her from the gray realm. Otherwise what was the point? A brain turned to mush and a cellular breakdown wouldn't do anyone any good.

He pushed the door open and disappeared inside, leaving it to slowly click back into place as he glanced around. His breaths blew out in long mists and his nostrils flared. It was cold in here with nothing but metal and tile and death.

Three bodies were laid out in a neat row along the far wall, their forms shrouded in shit-beige cotton. It was the one dash of color on an otherwise sterile, stainless steel canvas. He snorted and wondered if the moneyed folk knew that the death rate at the Regent seemed to be a little on the high side.

Logan crossed the room and drew back the cover on the first. It was a woman. Pale, lifeless eyes stared up at him, the faded brown already turning into the milky shade of death. Her hair was gray, knotted and thin, the skin wrinkled with age. Kira Dove was twenty-five. He covered her up and glanced at the next body.

The shape beneath the cover was large and long, suggesting someone close to three hundred pounds. He was going to guess that the little imp he remembered was not anywhere near that in stature.

Out of the blue her face flashed in his mind. Huge, dark, exotic eyes—almond in shape—with long, tangled ebony hair, and a little bow mouth that was as red as an apple.

She'd not been frightened when he'd appeared in her room. Not at first. In fact, he'd been more than a little surprised at the curiosity he'd sensed as she stared at him. She'd had no idea what the hell he was—how could she? The girl had only been ten. Yet most humans were scared shitless when he appeared—his hellhound form was intimidating, to say the least—and those with blackened souls knew exactly what he was.

And why he'd come.

Logan shook the memory from his mind and walked past the large body. He reached for the last one and yanked back the cover. It was the girl, of that he had no doubt.

Bruises covered the entire left side of her face and dried blood crusted near her nose and mouth. Her dark eyebrows were arched, delicate accents to adorn large eyes—which were not open. The long hair he remembered was no more—only hacked-off blunt ends remained, which barely touched her shoulders. The deep black color was gone, though the roots showed an inch thick among the

cheap blond dye job. Her skin held the sickly tinge of in-
doors, as if she'd not seen the sun in years, yet her body
was lean and muscular. The girl had worked out.

Hard.

Her arms lay at her sides and he noted scars along the
inside of her wrists. Some were fresh but a lot were old.
This girl had tried to die. Many times, by the looks of it.

Logan frowned. Why was she so damn important?

*Why had he been dispatched to drag her to hell when
she was ten?* Nothing about that night had been on
the up-and-up. His lips thinned and he scowled at the
memory. It had been all wrong. He'd known it then and
as he stared down at her broken body, something stirred
within him. Cold, anger, and something else.

It was the something else he dismissed. He had no
time for softness. For second-guessing. For fucking feel-
ings.

Logan bent low, closed his eyes, and inhaled deeply.
He filtered out the smell of death, of disinfectant and fear,
and growled as two scents rose to the fore.

Her unique signature he remembered with clarity—
which was odd, considering he'd targeted hundreds of
thousands of souls in his lifetime. The little Dove was still
full of honey and of the sun—surprisingly something
that had not been killed while she'd languished here in
this hellhole.

It was the other that had his hackles rising—the scent
of otherworld. It carried the unmistakable trace of the
upper realm.

Kira Dove had been murdered by one of Askelon's

own. But who? And why? He let the scent settle in his mind, compartmentalized the bastard's signature so he'd never forget. If he ever crossed paths with the murderer he'd know it.

He straightened and cocked his head down at her, a frown burrowing his forehead. The bruising on her arms and knuckles suggested she'd fought back, which was interesting, considering she'd had a death wish for years.

After a few moments, Logan covered the body with the sheet and took a step back—he had everything he needed. One more glance around and then he disappeared, his tall, muscled form changing shape as the beast inside erupted.

He charged past the startled receptionist, a blur of fur, fangs, and deadly intent. Outside he turned and headed toward the far corner of the estate. Once he was hidden deep within the gnarled overhang of bush that lined the edge of a swamp, he stopped.

Flanks heaving, the hellhound turned its head toward the dark sky and howled. The terrifying lament echoed into the stillness, reverberating and thickening as it traveled beyond.

It was a call that wouldn't go unanswered.

Within minutes a shadowed figure appeared, one that drifted above the ground. It was embraced within an ethereal mist that trailed behind it as it moved toward Logan, and when it was inches from the hellhound it stopped.

Why have you summoned me? The gatekeeper's rasp echoed inside Logan's mind.

Logan's blood-red eyes regarded the cloaked figure for a few moments and then he growled, their wordless conversation continuing.

You will let me pass into the gray realm.

The gatekeeper laughed. *Impossible. The gray realm is not for your kind.*

Logan moved forward—the hellhound's impressive height and muscled frame towering over the gatekeeper—and bared his teeth. *You will let me pass or I will hunt the daughter that you hide among the humans.*

The gatekeeper was shocked into silence and Logan watched him closely. Everyone had secrets. In his line of work it boded well to know as many as he could. Just as Bill had used Logan's own secret to force him into this covert mission, he'd use whatever he had in his back pocket to get it done.

Logan Winters would do whatever it took to keep his mother safe—she was the one thing he treasured above all else.

After several long moments, mist whirled around them both, cool tendrils slithering along the damp ground like spectral fingers. *Follow me.* The order was terse. Angry.

Logan charged forward on the heels of the gatekeeper and seconds later the gray mist swallowed them whole.

Chapter Three

KIRA DOVE HAD died and gone to heaven, or at the very least this was the closest she was going to get.

She stood in the middle of an open-air market surrounded by all sorts of vendors. They lined the square in a series of thatched roofs varying in shades of burnished gold to a dark brown tobacco color. Above her an azure blue sky blanketed as far as she could see, broken only by the odd cotton-candy cloud.

The stalls were filled to the brim with exotic fruits, clothes, colorful souvenirs, and—as an unmistakable melody in the wind greeted her ears and her smile widened—wind chimes. The kiss of sun caressed her face and the smell of the Caribbean tickled her nostrils.

A sense of déjà vu rushed through her, as if she'd been here before. But that was impossible, wasn't it?

She glanced around once more, brow furled in concentration. It did remind her of . . . of that place. . . . She bit her lip, puzzled. It reminded her of something, but at the moment she couldn't remember what that something was. Which was weird, wasn't it?

Kira turned in a full circle, smiling at the people milling about—families, friends, and lovers—and shrugged. She didn't care where she was, because who knew how long it was going to last?

All around her people moved about, buying wares hawked by pleasant-looking folks—they were as varied as the goods being offered for sale—men, women, black and white. Small animals ran past her feet—a white and gold dog chased by a tiny orange tabby. The animals wove around the crowd and disappeared, two small children close on their heels. The kids giggled and shouted in excitement as several youngsters appeared and joined them.

There was nothing dark or sinister about this place. No fear. She thought of Doctor Mergerone and bit her lip.

No pain.

She took a step and felt the gentle swish of something soft against her skin. She could have sworn she'd been wearing the ugly green uniform from the Institute—a baggy t-shirt and shorts—yet her fingers smoothed pale yellow silk over her hips.

It was the softest thing she'd ever touched and her fingers lingered, enjoying the feel.

She glanced down at her legs, eyes wide in wonder. Unbelievable. Gone was her pasty white skin—the only shade she'd ever remembered having—and instead, she was flush with golden health.

A breeze rolled through the market, whipping long

strands of her dark hair around her head. She tugged it from her eyes and grinned.

It felt silky. It felt smooth. There was no hint of dullness or dirt. Or knots. She shuddered.

Or bugs.

Kira took a few hesitant steps and halted, suddenly unsure.

Something nagged at her. It was a sliver of apprehension—a feeling that things weren't right—but she quickly buried it as an older woman motioned toward her.

"Come here, dear."

The woman wore a colorful dress that held every jewel tone imaginable woven into the threads. The skirt was full and swept the cobblestones in a rainbow cloud of cotton that reminded her of the gypsy folk her parents would hire to entertain at parties—vagabonds and free spirits. Her silken white hair flowed past her shoulders in gentle waves, and her kind eyes—the color of which Kira couldn't make out—were crinkled as she smiled.

Kira glanced around, not sure if the woman was looking at her or someone else—but there was no one there. In fact there wasn't much of anything behind the woman and her stall. It was weird. She saw shapes that appeared to be buildings of some sort, but they were lost in a gray mist that the sun didn't seem able to penetrate.

It was as if the market was the only thing that existed, but how could that be?

She bit her lip and paused as a man and his children passed in front of her. The youngest—a boy who looked to be about five, with a head full of golden curls and the bluest eyes she'd ever seen—glanced up at Kira and opened his mouth. No words came out but she shuddered as a whisper caressed her ear. *You don't belong here.*

For a second her vision blurred and she stumbled. She blinked and shook her head as the odd feeling persisted, but when she was able to focus there was no one there.

What the hell?

"Would you like a drink?" The musical sound of the old woman's voice drew Kira's attention and she quickly crossed the street, though she paused and hazarded a glance back. Just to be sure.

"Did you see them?" Kira's hand went to her throat in surprise. There was no rasp, no weakness from an ill-used voice box. She sounded strong, if a little unsure.

The woman stirred a large, colorful drink inside a glass so cold moisture collected along its sides and ran down in small rivulets. She shrugged. "There are a lot of souls here. Some I see," she glanced up at Kira and winked, "and some I don't." She handed the magenta-colored drink to Kira. "You, I see."

Kira accepted the glass, though she wasn't quite sure she should drink it.

"Go ahead." The kind eyes stared up at her. "Drink. It will make things clearer."

At the woman's urging, Kira took a long draw of the cool liquid. Tangy and sweet at the same time, she gulped it down, smiling and more than a little embarrassed as she wiped a drop from the corner of her mouth.

"Sorry, I'm so thirsty all of a sudden." She arched a brow. "Can I have a bit more?"

The woman shook her head. "Sorry. I can only give you one drink."

"Oh," Kira murmured, her cheeks darkening as an awkward silence fell between them. "I'm . . ." A wave of thirst rolled over her. "I'm just so thirsty."

The woman nodded. "Most are when they first arrive. The drink will help."

"Arrive?" Something pricked along the edge of her mind. A memory. A dark one that came with cold and fear and pain. She pushed it away. She didn't want to remember.

"I've not seen you before. You're new." The woman clucked like she was talking to a child, and Kira blushed.

"I'm sorry if I seem to be a bit confused. What's your name?" Kira asked.

The woman opened her mouth and then closed it, her eyebrows knit in concentration. She stared up at Kira for so long that Kira began to feel uncomfortable.

Then she smiled widely and nodded. "Catherine."

"Oh," Kira felt her heart lurch. Catherine had been her nana's name, though her nana had insisted she call her—

"You can call me Cat."

Cat. Kira's eyes narrowed and she took a step backward. This was too much of a coincidence.

She studied the small woman who stood in silence with a wide smile plastered to her face. Something was way off. She bit her lip nervously and looked around, thinking she'd been a fool to accept a drink from the woman.

"Where am I?" she asked, heart beating heavy and voice strained.

Catherine—*Cat*—smiled and crooked her head to the side. "Why, my dear, you're where you're supposed to be . . . for the moment."

"But where is that, exactly?" It was hard for Kira to keep the frustration from her voice as she glanced around. Palm trees wavered along the edge of the market, their leaves brushing the tops of the stalls, their stems whispering in the breeze. Had they been there before?

"It's where you need to be."

The woman was talking in circles. Kira ran fingers through the long hair at her neck and then paused, her hands in the air. The marks were gone. All of them.

She turned both of her wrists over and swallowed as her stomach roiled. Shame darkened her cheeks as the image of her scars flashed before her eyes. They were reminders of her pain and weakness.

And they were no more.

"What's happening?" she whispered.

Why was she missing a huge chunk of time? Why was she not back at the Institute? Her eyebrows knit together and she shook her head. The last thing she remembered was . . . Mergerone and the two new orderlies coming into her room.

Kira's heart thudded heavily and a wave of heat suffused her cheeks. Her chest was tight and it was hard to breathe. She looked at Catherine and opened her mouth to speak, but something shifted then and she froze.

A trace of energy rippled through the market, touching everything and electrifying the air. The sky darkened and the sun that she'd dreamt about for so long disappeared behind dark, thunderous clouds.

"I don't understand." Fear clogged her throat and she was barely able to get the words out.

The woman moved forward, her frail body quick, preternatural. Her gnarled hands ensconced Kira's tight within her grasp. "Your memories will come back. It's different with everyone." The old woman's hand was on her cheek, the touch light. "The drink will help."

A frown crossed Catherine's face as her gaze drifted behind Kira. Something flickered behind their glittery depths. She murmured something in a language that Kira didn't understand and then grasped both of her wrists tightly, her eyes intense as she looked up at Kira.

"They are not supposed to be here."

"Who?" Kira whirled around but all she saw were the same tourists milling about. A flash of blond caught her eye and for a second she thought she saw the little boy from moments earlier, but then he was gone.

"Kira."

She turned back to the old woman. "You need to follow the light." Catherine pointed behind her. "Understand?"

Hell, no. I think you're crazier than I am.

"I don't . . ." Kira shook her head helplessly.

"You need to go now." Catherine's voice changed and Kira jerked her head up. Cat nodded. "Now." She nodded behind her. "Toward the light."

Kira took a few steps past the old woman, but paused as thunder joined the lightning now crossing the sky. The tourists walked about the market as if unaware that everything had changed. They laughed among themselves, hands reaching for fantastic bargains as they chatted animatedly.

For the first time she noticed that not everyone was dressed the same. Some wore clothes that looked to be from centuries ago—velvet and silk ball gowns, top hats, and powdered wigs. There was a woman dressed smartly in a simple dress cut to just above the knee and a royal blue pin hat. At her throat was a thick strand of pearls, and white kid gloves adorned her hands. She looked like she was from the 1960s. None of this made sense.

Kira blinked rapidly. Now that she'd taken a moment to look closer, some of the tourists didn't even look human.

Where the hell did that thought come from?

She turned around and a chill rolled over her. Two shadowy figures stood at the edge of the square. They were tall, well over six feet in height, with wide shoulders and powerful arms. They were dressed in long robes that billowed around their feet, dancing in a breeze that seemed not to touch anyone else.

Their faces weren't clear and in fact the hoods they wore seemed to hide nothing but dark space. They moved forward slowly, their heads turning in unison as if an invisible rope tethered them together. As they perused the market, something about the way they moved sent panic crashing through Kira.

They were unnatural. *Just like the monster from her*

childhood. A flash of fur and fangs and the sensation of heat erupted in her mind.

Their feet didn't touch the ground, and the air shimmered around them as they started toward the market.

And yet, no one seemed to notice them. A young woman jogged in place as she reached for a basket of fruit, her caramel-blond hair held in place by a bright pink band. An elderly man shuffled along slowly, his cane tapping the cobblestone at his feet as he sang a strange tune. The dog reappeared once more, its yipping accelerated as it dove into the crowd.

In that moment everything expanded and then constricted into a tight beam of energy. The world was off-kilter and Kira had no idea what the hell was going on.

"Go, now." Catherine's voice was urgent and this time Kira didn't hesitate.

Follow the light.

Kira kept her head down and ran toward an alley just behind Catherine's market stall. She slipped between the walls and paused, glancing back toward the square once she was hidden in the shadows.

Something thick and dull pounded against her skull and her gut churned in fear. Confusion didn't even come close to describing the images that haunted her head. The things that had driven her mad years before rose to the surface and Kira backed away as the two shadows converged at the end of the alley.

They effectively cut off any means of escape, and for a second Kira struggled to see past the darkness that seeped from beneath their robes, pouring out like thick billowing clouds of smoke. She tried to speak but her vocal cords froze, and her hands clenched so tightly she drew blood.

The specter on the left made a screeching noise and pointed its arm toward her. "You." Its disembodied voice cut through her brain. It hurt.

She jumped as a growl erupted behind her. Kira whirled around and her fist flew to her mouth as she tried to squelch the scream that caught at the back of her throat.

A man stood, his tall length cloaked in shadow, though his eyes burned through the darkness, a fierce red that cut through the gloom.

She knew those eyes. She knew them well. They belonged to her savior—or at least that's what she called him. How many nights had she dreamed of him? Of seeing him again? Of touching him? Of losing herself in his embrace?

As a child he'd been nothing more than a memory to cling to. Something that was real in a world of chaos and pain. Yet as she grew older, stuck in the hellhole that was the Institute, the way she thought of him had changed.

When her world had spiraled out of control it was him she'd turned to. Her angel. Her savior. Mergerone had come for her again and again, drugging her, hurting her . . . touching her . . . and it was the stranger and his strength that had gotten her through.

Oh my God. It was all real. What the doctors called delusions were in fact real. She wasn't crazy.

A tremulous smile claimed her lips, but faded just as quickly because she knew that if *he* was back, then maybe the beast wasn't far behind.

Kira Dove had slipped down a rabbit hole fifteen years ago and it seemed as if the ghosts that haunted her head had found her once more.

No longer were they spectral nightmares that kept her awake. They were real.

And they were coming for her.

Chapter Four

KIRA UNCLENCHED HER hands and forced the tense muscles that stretched across her shoulders to relax. She needed her head clear and her body loose, ready to fight.

There was a certain amount of anticipation tingling along her nerves that made her jumpy. She'd be a fool not to recognize what the adrenaline pumping through her veins meant.

She'd somehow always known that the events of that long-ago night had been real. They'd not been the imaginings of a girl gone crazy.

That's what had driven her to the brink so many times. It's what fueled her suicide attempts. As much as the memory of the beast had pushed her to train and prepare to fight, it had also fed the fear inside of her. And that's what had almost made her as crazy as everyone thought she was.

Kira tore her eyes from the nameless man and whirled

back toward the two specters, a smile widening her face. To have proof—absolute knowledge that she'd been right—was enough. The mad ramblings of doomsday and fire and Armageddon had been bang-on. It brought some small sliver of peace.

Even now the pain and frustration she'd felt at the poorly hidden disappointment and denial in her parents' eyes hit her hard in the gut. They wouldn't listen to anyone—not even her beloved nana, Catherine.

They'd called in all sorts of specialists, the best that money could buy, from every corner of the globe, and pummeled them with questions. What's wrong with her? Will she be normal again? Is she crazy?

Their answers had been as varied as the doctors. She's delusional. She's psychotic. She's dangerous.

After six months of trying to *fix* their now-broken child, Andre and Miriam Dove had tossed her aside and left her to rot in the Institute. They'd come to visit at first, but after months of no improvement the visits had dwindled and eventually stopped. Her nana had never been *allowed* to visit.

Every birthday from her eleventh on had been spent in that hellhole. No longer was Kira the perfect blending of the Doves' fabulous genes. She was damaged. Deranged.

Yet she was stronger than any of them. Not once had she accepted the diagnosis—even as young as she was. The doctors had tried all sorts of "therapies" to get through to her. Some were passive but most involved some sort of pain.

When she was nineteen, a new specialist arrived at

the Institute—one who seemed invested in her case. Dr. Mergerone had been inventive and took perverse pleasure in "treating" her.

Kira had never given in. She'd known her savior was real.

The beast existed.

She'd known the beast would return for her—she'd seen him in dreams, among other things. Kira knew bad tidings were coming as surely as she knew the sun would rise each day. They'd hidden inside shadows that twisted in the corners and fell to her ears as whispers in the night. Images of destruction and pain had haunted her every night for as long as she had memory.

Sometimes it had been too much and she'd retreated deep into her mind, her physical body in a catatonic state as she grappled with what she saw. Her savior. The beast. A child.

And now, for the first time in years, the fog had lifted. All those moments of clarity—when she'd trained hard, pushed her body until collapse—had been important. She needed to be strong.

She had to survive.

One of the specters spoke, a high-pitched sound as piercing as a thousand cicadas singing off key. The words made no sense and she struggled to understand even as she wanted to cover her ears and hide.

"I want you the hell out of here, now."

Kira's heart nearly fell from her chest as she jerked to the left. He was there. The savior. Inches away.

"I won't. I can't leave you." How could she? She would fight by his side. It's what she'd trained for.

His eyes no longer burned red and the shadows melted away, giving her a glimpse of his face.

In all her imaginings, both as a young girl and later as a woman, she'd never seen his face. It had always been the eyes—those blood-red eyes—that had burned within her memories.

And oh, what she'd been missing.

He was breathtaking. He was hard and masculine and wild and big. He was the tallest man she'd ever seen in person, easily topping six feet by several inches. Dressed in black denim and a tight-fitting black t-shirt, he presented an intimidating figure. His jaw was shadowed in several days of scruff, and thick, black hair waved down to his collar.

He had strong cheekbones and a nose that was slightly imperfect—as if it had been broken at least once. Or twice. His lips were full and for a second her eyes lingered there.

He scowled and hissed loudly, taking two steps forward until he was abreast of her.

"I wasn't asking. Unless you want your ass kicked but good, you need to leave."

Too bad his attitude sucked.

"Says who?" Anger flashed inside Kira, the kind that burned as it went down.

He looked surprised at her retort and his lips tightened in anger.

She glanced back toward the two robed figures. They

floated several inches off the ground and their robes billowed out even farther, the silky ends widening until they touched either side of the alley's muted orange brick walls. Dark, smoky mist continued to slither from beneath their robes, and newly discernible shapes moved among the murky fog.

There was no rational explanation for what she was seeing, and yet, she accepted it.

"I'm not going anywhere." She stood with her legs spread, balancing on the balls of her feet as she squared her shoulders. For the first time in *forever*, she felt like she was standing at the helm of the ship that was her life. She could steer it. She was strong enough.

"You can't fight them on your own." She gestured toward the robed figures. "You need me."

He laughed—which pissed her off. "Do I look like I need your help?"

Really? He was going to pick a fight now?

"You look like an arrogant son of a bitch, if you want the truth." She arched a brow. "Who the hell are you, anyway? Should I just call you 'caveman'? You have a Neanderthal complex or what?"

She almost cracked a smile at the thunderous look that crossed his face.

"I don't have time for this," he hissed, and leaned closer. "Leave now or else."

She crossed her arms and lifted her chin. The man was hard-edged, arrogant, and very, very pissed off.

But so was Kira. She was sick and tired of living in

the shadows. Of cowering in fear and hiding from the unknown.

"Or else what?" She was strangely exhilarated.

For a moment they stared at each other—David against Goliath—and then a screech erupted, one that shattered the moment like a hammer smashing against stone.

Kira tore her eyes from his and glanced toward the entrance to the alley. The shapes beneath the specters' robes rose up, long plumes of smoke that twisted faster and faster still, until they solidified into creatures that she'd never seen before. Not even in her nightmares.

There were six in total—tall, thin, hulking things with arms that bounced in front of them as if tethered from above by a puppeteer. They were as faceless as the creatures that had born them, but fire flashed from where eyes should be and large gaping holes appeared as they screeched once more.

Maggots surged from their mouths, twisting, turning, and falling to the ground as the smoke monsters moved forward en masse. The squirming maggots began to multiply when they hit the ground, and soon there was a teeming mass of hundreds, if not thousands of the slimy things.

Her belly roiled at the sight.

Caveman stepped in front of her, a snarl falling from his lips as he shoved her aside. "For fuck's sake, why won't you listen to me? This isn't a game."

Kira had to make him understand. "I'm not afraid."

She inched forward until she was so close that she could reach out and touch him. "Not anymore."

He glanced over his shoulder and she froze at the look on his face. His eyes burned blood red once more and for a second she could have sworn she glimpsed something savage in their depths.

He both scared the crap out of her and tugged at something deep inside. At emotions long buried. Need. Want. In that moment Kira would have done anything to stay by his side. To fight with him. To touch him.

To kiss him.

Her hand rose of its own accord and she paused, wondering if the swell of emotion inside was because she was close to death.

She felt that too—death—like a cold, lingering memory that wouldn't go away. It didn't matter. None of it did anymore. There was only the here and now. This man and their common enemy.

"I won't leave you." She grabbed his arm and the roaring in her ears dialed down. His skin was taut beneath her fingers, his flesh burning hot, so very hot.

He hissed and inhaled sharply but didn't pull away.

Kira's breaths fell in short, painful spurts as her chest tightened. For several moments there was only the air escaping her lungs and the crazy beating of her heart. There were the small, curling hairs along his forearm and the shifting, corded muscles beneath.

There was his heat. His smell. His intensity.

Her eyes moved upward. She saw the thin sheen of

sweat that coated his skin. The pulse that beat just as fast and hard as her own.

When their eyes connected once more, she was shocked at the look on his face. It was something dark and disturbing.

Suddenly he didn't look anything like the man of moments before. He looked inhuman.

He snarled and bared his teeth.

She wretched her hand away and stepped back.

"Smart girl." He said savagely. "You say you're not afraid?" He gestured toward the smoke creatures that were almost upon them. "They're nothing like what I am."

His skin shifted, shadows flickering across his face as his eyes blazed at her. "What are you?" Kira whispered.

The man she'd called savior for the last fifteen years rolled his shoulders and spoke coldly. "I'll be your worst nightmare if you don't listen to me and get the hell out of here."

Fire and sulfur filled her nostrils and the rumbling that erupted from his chest was menacing. He sounded like an animal.

Kira blinked and a chill rolled over her at the smile that sat upon his face as he gazed at the smoke creatures. He looked like he wanted to rip them apart . . . with his bare hands.

The screeching had ramped up considerably and the noise was near deafening. How the people in the market didn't hear was a bloody miracle, and yet no one else had come to her rescue.

"Run the other way and don't stop until you have to."

"But," Kira glanced backward. "But there's nothing there. The alley ends."

He swore under his breath. Or at least Kira assumed it was some sort of curse word—it sure as hell wasn't any language she'd ever heard before.

"You need to trust me and go. A door will open. It always does in a place like this."

One of the smoke creatures broke formation and rushed toward them.

"Now!" He shouted, pushing her behind him as he lunged forward, an eerie howl echoing into the night as he did so. "I will find you."

"But why are you here?" None of this made sense. "Where is here?"

"Lady, we don't have time for twenty questions."

Kira hesitated, suddenly not sure about anything anymore.

"If you don't get your ass out of here I'll kill you myself."

Something in his tone scared her far more than the smoke creatures. She whirled around and took off, running as fast as she could until she reached the end of the alley. Boxes were stacked to the left of her, and on the right . . . she looked closer . . . was the wall moving?

The brick liquefied and warped, moaning in protest as an opening appeared, and from behind it, the soft glow of light peaked through.

Follow the light.

What was this place? She must be dreaming. There could be no other explanation.

Another screech ripped through the night, but this time it was followed by a roar that sent shivers racing across her flesh. It was ugly and full-bodied—filled with a darkness she was familiar with.

Dream or no dream, it was enough to get her butt moving. She plunged into the unknown and didn't look back.

Chapter Five

KIRA DOVE'S SCENT lingered in the air, a tantalizing fragrance that teased his nostrils. It held the merest whisper of honey, but was enough to point Logan in the right direction.

He cracked his neck and rolled his shoulders, wincing at the pain that lashed across his muscles. The damn smoke creatures had proved harder to kill than he'd thought they'd be, and the extra time he'd dealt with them kept him that much farther away from his target.

He'd been afraid that Kira's scent would fade, that the gray realm would shift and it would take him too long to find her again.

Luckily for him he'd been able follow her path from the alley, though he wasn't entirely sure where he was at the moment.

He turned, a muscle working its way sharply across his jaw as a frown stole over his features. His arm still tingled from her touch—the flash of heat and need still roiled beneath his flesh. In all of his years, he'd never felt such a connection—such an insane desire to take, to hold, and to claim. Not even when he'd fancied the werewolf, Lita.

What the hell was up with that?

His eyes narrowed as he searched the gloom; her energy left small signatures behind, little bits of her soul that glistened among the shadows. He saw them there, drifting up ahead, like magical fireflies. They were beacons of light in the darkness as surely as if she'd lit the path with a hundred torches.

Behind him, the market had been swallowed whole—sucked into one of the many invisible threads of existence that shifted and changed constantly here. It's what made purgatory so dangerous. The gray realm was constantly changing, combining bits of a person's reality and bits of what the realm was—which, to most, was a mystery.

Many had been lost here for millennia, especially the ones who didn't belong.

Like him.

Logan rolled his shoulders and moved forward, pushing any thought but retrieval from his mind. Damned if he was going to stay any longer than he had to. He'd grab the girl, find his way back to the portal, and get the hell out. Once she was back in Bill's custody he could forget all about Kira Dove.

He slid among the shadows with predatory ease. Out here along the edges of the gray realm it was quiet, though the landscape was ever-changing. Buildings rose up on either side of him—tall, monstrous things that disappeared in the clouds—and down the way a carnival was in progress; a massive Ferris wheel slowly turned, though no one rode it.

A gentle breeze stirred bits of paper and large orange leaves that had come from nowhere. They danced in front of him, lingering in the air, before being swept away behind him.

The street before him was eerily quiet save for a lone soul several feet ahead of him. The man paused, swiveling his head around until he spied Logan.

His clothing was not the modern type that Logan had come to prefer—jeans and t-shirt had been his mode of dress for years. This man, his clothing spoke of a different time.

A top hat sat precariously on his head and his facial hair was elegant—a mustache neatly trimmed with a salt-and-pepper beard to match. Round glasses perched on an overly long, thin nose gave him a bit of a hawkish look. His overcoat was royal blue; at his throat a crisp, starched shirt; and his white pants, showing stains on the knees, were tucked into brown leather knee-high boots.

In his hand he clutched a riding crop, his fingers covered with dirty gloves that at one time must have been white, yet now were dove gray.

The man tipped his head and tapped his hat. "I say, sir, can you point me toward . . ." He frowned. "I'm just looking for the . . ." His voice trailed off and he cleared his throat, embarrassed. "Sorry . . . lately I seem to have difficulty remembering what exactly it is I'm looking for."

He arched a brow hopefully, a sad, wistful smile claiming his mouth.

"Sorry, I can't help you with that." Logan's words were clipped.

Poor bastard. Logan wondered how many more years he was doomed to wander, never resting, always searching for the path that would lead him to salvation.

"Oh yes, well," the man crooked his head to the side and touched the edge of his top hat, "a good day to you then, sir." Shoulders slumped, the man continued on his way and soon disappeared into the heavy mist that rolled across the pavement.

Logan followed in his steps, his gaze locked on to the thinning whispers of light that danced in the air. He crossed the street, nostrils flaring as the girl's scent sharpened and then faded.

Where the hell was she?

Logan paused, closed his eyes, and concentrated. He inhaled great gulps of air, his body analyzing every particle, tearing them apart, and seconds later he turned. The billowing clouds of mist faded and there across the way was a massive forest. He sensed many creatures hidden behind the trees: lost souls, spirit guides, and more than a few who didn't belong.

His chest grumbled and he bared his teeth. His human girl was wandering among them.

Logan took off at a run and plunged headlong into the thick stand of trees. They were taller than any found in the human realm, great soldiers made of ancient wood that had stood guard for millennia, their eyes watching in silence the parade of souls doomed to wander the gray realm.

In here, deep within their ranks, was an entirely different world. The quiet was heavy, the scents fresh and sharp. A healthy dose of greenery lay at his feet—tall grasses, weeds, and bushes—and the rich scent of freshly mown lawn reached his nostrils.

What the hell? He supposed nothing should surprise him, but still . . .

Logan turned to the left and slipped deeper into the forest, his eyes catching small twists of energy that dissolved in the air just as quickly as they appeared. Overhead a crimson moon shone, casting an eerie glow that penetrated through the trees until it reached the forest floor and bathed the underbrush in red.

He began to jog, zigzagging among the maze of trees. She was close by—he could feel it.

A few moments later the trees gave way to a clearing and he stopped abruptly. The drone of a lawn mower echoed, but the sound was thick instead of sharp, as if muted. A large balding man sat atop a massive red contraption, humming a tune, as a gold and white dog and kitten ran behind it. Perfect green rows that crisscrossed in an elegant pattern lay before him. It was a veritable masterpiece, if you were into landscaping.

Yeah, that looked about right, cutting the grass at night under a blood-red moon . . . in the middle of a park.

Welcome to the gray realm.

The man glanced up, smiled and waved, and then

pointed toward a white pavilion in the distance, near the edge of the forest. The Dove girl was there. Alone.

He reached the pavilion just as she turned.

"You found me."

"I told you I would."

"I've learned that most men are liars." She stared down at him and her eyes narrowed. "I don't understand any of this. You need to explain things to me."

Logan studied the girl and realized a few things. First off, she wasn't a girl—there was nothing remotely childish about the woman who stared down at him. Her long dark hair blew in the breeze and her features, while pale, were exceptional—large almond-shaped eyes in a shade of chocolate that was hard to describe, delicate nose, and small, generous mouth. And though she was slender, she filled out a dress the way a woman should—with high, firm breasts, a narrow waist, and soft, rounded hips.

He felt a modicum of relief. Had he reacted to Kira simply because her beauty called to him? Was that all it was?

He thought of the broken body at the morgue with the chopped-off hair, gaunt face, and dried blood—the bruises, scarred wrists, and broken bones. That was Kira Dove's reality. This was nothing more than a fantasy, and sadly, she didn't know it yet.

It was a lie. All of it.

An owl hooted in the distance, breaking the silence, its sad, lonely call echoing eerily in the air. Logan turned toward the forest. Something slithered among the trees, several hundred feet away. His nostrils flared—it wasn't friendly. The stink of otherworld was all over it.

He didn't have time to hold her hand and tell her everything was going to be all right. He needed to get her the hell out of the park and out of the gray realm, back to the shit reality she'd been stolen from. Bill could deal with her from there and leave both him and his mother the hell out of it.

"We need to leave." His tone was brusque and he motioned for her to follow. The trojan demons and the smoke creatures they'd borne had been handled easily by him. Child's play, really. But Logan knew the big guns would be dispatched as soon as word reached whoever it was that wanted the girl dead that a hellhound was loose in the gray realm—one with a claim on the human.

He couldn't risk losing her. Not with the fate of his mother at hand.

He glanced up at her once more, took stock of the squared shoulders and chin thrust out in defiance. "You don't listen well, do you?" Logan took a step closer.

"Do you know what this place is?" She turned in a circle, arms outstretched, totally oblivious to the danger hidden in the shadows.

"Looks like a patch of grass and some trees to me."

"No." She nailed him with an intense look. "No, it's not. I've seen it before." Her brow furled and his gaze settled on her lips as a small tongue darted out. "In magazines, just like I saw the market. Every detail is the same. I used to fantasize about losing myself in those places." She tucked an errant strand of hair behind her ear and shook her head. "Back at the . . ." She rubbed her forehead and bit her lip. "Back at that place." A smile crossed her face. "Back at the Institute." She finished triumphantly.

He remained silent, though he was aware of the shadows shifting beyond his line of sight.

"That man? Cutting the grass?" She exhaled a long, shuddering breath. "I know him . . . I mean, I *knew* him. He was a groundskeeper at the Regent." She watched the man for a few seconds, a faint smile on her face. "He was nice to me. I was never allowed outside but sometimes I'd manage to sneak away. All I wanted was to be free, you know?" She shook her head and whispered. "I'd go months without feeling the sun on my face, or smelling the salt of the ocean. Occasionally I'd find a way to sneak outside. He'd see me but pretend he didn't. He'd lie for me. If I was lucky, Mergerone wouldn't find me for hours."

"That's nice. Now can we go?" Logan took a step up onto the pavilion. He'd damn well pull her down if he had to.

"You don't understand."

"I understand more than you know."

She pointed to grass-cutting man once more. "He died a few years ago. Mergerone couldn't wait to tell me. So why is he here? Why am I here?" Her voice rose several notches. "How could I have been at a market in the Caribbean and in Central Park within an hour of each other? On what planet is that possible?"

A dark sliver of energy materialized on the far side of the park. Logan growled and took the last step until he was inches from her. "Look, lady. We don't have time for tea and cookies and twenty-five fucking questions."

She totally ignored him, which pissed him off. Usually when Logan's animal rumbled beneath his flesh, people took notice.

"You rescued me from that . . . that thing all those years ago. I remember all of it. I *know* you too."

That surprised him.

"You brought me back from the dark place. You saved me from the beast."

"The beast?" He snorted. If she only knew.

Her eyes were liquid pools and she nodded slowly. "Yes, the beast. At least that's what I call it." She paused. "I thought of you as my savior for the longest time, but that's not what you are, is it?"

"No."

She paused and then whispered. "So what are you?"

He watched her closely. "The beast."

"You're full of shit." Damn but she had spunk.

"Am I?"

She opened her mouth to speak, but then closed it as fear entered her eyes. It amused Logan that she thought him a savior, and yet at the same time, she looked so damn lost that . . . that what? He thought he could help? He *wanted* to help? Did he think a hug and a kiss on the cheek was going to make everything all right?

First off, he didn't do hugs, and secondly . . . did he really want to go there?

Angrily Logan inched forward. He had no time for

bullshit. The shadows that crept along the edge of the park were now tenfold. The time for games was over.

"Kira," he began, surprised at how easily her name rolled off his lips. She took another step and backed away from him.

"Stay away from me."

"I can't do that. I was sent to bring you back and I'm not leaving here without you." He let that sink in. "So, listen up. You see those shadows over there?" He pointed toward the far edge of the park and waited until she turned to look. "Those are trojans. They're slaves to otherworld creatures of great power, and if they're here it means their master isn't far behind. They'll keep coming for you until . . ."

He was so close to her he could count the lashes that feathered her eyes. For a few seconds he stared down at her—inhaling her fear and confusion.

His voice trailed off and he grabbed her chin, slowly pulling her face up toward his. She licked her lips and for a second he was lost. Lost in her scent, in her warmth and the softness of her skin. He felt a pull, deep inside, a tug at the very heart of him—that place of darkness, and passion, and feral need.

Logan swallowed thickly. His body felt tight, as if his flesh was strung way too tight over bone and muscle. He itched and burned. His nostrils flared. *He* lusted . . . for *her*.

"Until what?"

His grip tightened. "Until they kill you . . . *again*," he

said softly. She wrenched her hand away, eyes wide with horror, and he knew that she was finally getting it.

"Oh God."

"God has nothing to do with it." Logan motioned for her to follow once more. There was no time to sugarcoat. "They've already killed you in the human realm but if they kill you here, in this place," he turned and gazed across the field, "your soul will be lost forever. And that is a punishment I wouldn't wish on my worst enemy."

Chapter Six

IMAGES PUMMELED HER brain. Fists. Knife. Leering faces and spittle. They echoed and hurt and split her mind into a thousand fragments of memory. Kira sagged against the man—she still didn't know his name—and moaned.

It was overwhelming. The thoughts. The pain. The fear.

Her stomach roiled and for a moment she thought she was going to be sick all over his heavy boots.

"Goddamn but I don't have time for this." His voice was sharp and she glanced up at him. His dark eyes burned red and his teeth were bared like an animal's.

"I don't," she couldn't articulate what was in her brain. How could she? Remembering the last moments of her life seemed an impossible thing, but it was there. The pictures, the sounds, the smells.

Mergerone's maniacal grin. His cold hands. The two orderlies who'd accompanied them. She groaned once more and would have staggered away, but two strong arms held her fast. "What they did . . ." She shook her head and closed her eyes. "What they did to me."

Oh my God, I'm dead. But how can that be? I'm alive . . . I think.

None of this made sense. Where the hell was she? And who was this man that held her?

"How is this possible? I mean, if I'm not really here, how can we be having a conversation?"

His hand was on her chin again—this time his touch was gentle, though the sound of his voice was anything but. He glared down at her. "There'll be time to process that shit later." He glanced up and swore. "Right now we have to disappear, and fast, understand?"

He hopped down from the pavilion, pulling Kira along with him. His muscles bunched beneath her fingers. There was strength there—real strength and not just the physical. She sensed he was made up of many layers—a lot were hidden, though she wasn't entirely sure she wanted to see them.

"What's your name?" Suddenly she dug her feet in, not even sure why it was so important. "In all this craziness I need to at least know that."

Kira waited, heart nearly beating out of her chest, fully aware of the shadows moving toward them, yet as she stared up into the dark eyes above her she felt . . . safe. She felt hope.

And for the first time in ages, here in this place of chaos, she felt a kind of . . . peace.

"Logan."

His one word answer was terse but it was enough to settle the demons inside, at least for the moment. He pushed her ahead of him and nodded toward the forest. "We need to find a place to hide until I can figure out how to get us back."

"So I'm not dead."

"That's a technicality that won't matter if we don't get the hell out of here."

He looked away, ignoring her, his lips tight, hands clenched.

"Wait a minute," she grabbed his arm again, though she let it go quickly as his face darkened into a scowl. "You don't know how to get us back? Seriously? How the hell do we know that's the right way to go?" She pointed toward the forest.

Disbelief crossed his features and he stopped cold. "You want to argue that point with me now?"

"No, I just thought you'd know—"

"Do us both a favor, all right? Don't think." He leaned in close and she shivered as the stubble along his chin grazed the flesh beneath her ear. His breath was warm, though his voice was cold as ice. He growled. "Run."

She was frozen, her feet rooted to the ground.

"Run, little Dove." This time the order was barked and Kira reacted instantly. Grass-cutting man pointed toward a fountain that seemed to have appeared from nowhere and she dashed toward it, Logan on her heels.

They were nearly to the fountain when Logan snarled, the sound so vicious the hair on the back of her neck stood on end. Kira spun around, watching in horror as several of the trojans gathered in a semicircle, while the largest in the pack advanced toward Logan.

They were ten feet in height—at least—and their bodies were made of leather-like skin in varying shades of silver. Overly large heads with luminescent eyes of teal, and teeth as sharp as a blade and as brown as the earth beneath her feet. The creatures stood upright, though it looked like they balanced themselves with long tails that swept out behind them and were covered in spikes the color of a blood-red harvest moon.

"You will die first, dog." The closest one to Logan spoke, the words slithered from between its green lips like syrup dripping from a bottle.

"Kira, run!" Logan barely got his words out before the creature rushed him. A blanket of energy surrounded Logan—Kira couldn't explain it any other way—and enveloped him whole. Small bursts of electricity sparked up into the air and a god-awful roar erupted from inside as the energy vortex swirled around him.

She took a step back and if she wasn't sure about anything before, she sure as hell had no clue what the hell was happening now. The energy dissipated like steam escaping a kettle; small puffs were there and then they were gone. She froze. Her mouth went dry and she struggled to breathe.

Logan was gone.

A massive hulking animal stared back at her with fiery red eyes and a thick, shaggy coat of fur—like burnt tobacco shot through with bolts of gold—and it was as large as the creatures before them.

It growled and swept its tail back and forth menacingly. Remnants of energy shimmered against its hide, slipping away and disappearing as it howled into the sky and turned toward the advancing trojans.

It was Logan.

It was the beast.

She shook her head and stifled a hysterical laugh. Isn't that what he'd told her?

What are you?

He turned to her once more and barked a low-timbered growl that sent shivers racing across her flesh. Kira took a step toward him even as everything inside screamed at her to flee. Her chest tightened, filled with the childhood fears she'd dreamt about for years. Was he her enemy? Or her savior?

The red eyes burned bright and the animal nodded its head. He wanted her to run, and yet . . . Kira still hesitated.

The trojans closest to Logan lunged, filling the evening air with a screech that was like chalk scraping along a blackboard, and Logan—or rather, the beast—met it halfway. The two bodies crashed together with a sickening thud and it was enough to shake her from the invisible hands that held her.

Kira took a step back, flexing her muscles and gathering the courage to run. The other creatures spread out along the side, effectively cutting off any escape for her. They hissed, the vibrations heavy in the air and licking across her body with a vibrato that made her skin crawl.

In the distance, grass-cutting man continued his solitary job, retracing the same rows she'd watched him trim not more than half an hour ago. A soft red glow from the moon bathed everything in red. It was surreal. It was unbelievable.

As O'Bannon, another patient at the Institute used to say . . . this place was a total mind fuck.

Kira didn't hesitate any longer. She whirled around, her feet flying over the grass as she dove for the fountain. The trojans were on either side, but if she was able to make it across the damn thing, she might have a chance at reaching the forest ahead of them.

Her long yellow skirt trailed out behind her and she felt a tug as she hopped over. Kira nearly fell to her knees as the fresh, cool water splashed up to her waist. It was much deeper than she'd anticipated and she righted herself, cursing as she struggled to gain her footing. The bottom of the fountain was made of hundreds, if not thousands, of shiny pennies, much like the ones her nana used to collect.

They shimmered beneath the surface, a burnt copper mirage, lit up by an incandescent light that came from nowhere. For a second she was mesmerized by them, but then the trojan closest to her reached for the edge of the fountain. Its long claw grasped the stone lip and made an eerie sound as its nails scraped along the top.

A song drifted to her then, a melodic kaleidoscope of notes, and the creature paused, momentarily entranced with the strange new sound. It came from a small truck that slowly made its way across the pristine park, and on its side bright pink letters that looked like candy cane clouds read, *Ice Cream Man*.

Another memory tugged at her. Hot summer afternoons, Ice Cream Man in his special truck with the song that drove her mother nuts.

She shook the memory from her mind and plunged forward, frowning as the water got deeper the farther along she got. Panic nipped at her heels. It was hard to make her way through.

Behind her the sounds that ripped into the night were loud enough to tear a hole the size of Texas into the atmosphere—they were brutal, primal.

She'd just cleared the large center sculpture—a massive replica of a cherub with water spouting out of its mouth—when she paused and turned around.

The remaining trojans had formed a circle around their leader and Logan . . . or the beast . . . or whatever the hell he was. She winced as a howl erupted from their midst.

Was it him? Logan?

Her foot slipped and Kira disappeared beneath the surface, unable to stop the pull that grabbed her legs and dragged her under. She looked up, hands flailing clumsily, but it was no use and she panicked as she began a downward descent.

Bubbles rose in front of her, small balls of air that came up to the surface like balloons in the sky. She watched them, a silent scream trapped in her throat. All kinds of thoughts rushed through her mind but one was foremost: if she was already dead . . . how could she die again?

That thought scared her more than anything and she began to thrash, though it did her no good. She kicked and clawed, and still she headed down into the darkness.

How deep was this fountain? Did it matter? She stopped moving and still she sank. Bubbles popped in front of her and she watched them rise as she headed in the other direction, pulled by some invisible force.

Kira's mind was chaotic, her head dizzy.

She saw Mergerone's cruel smile.

She saw her grandmother, Catherine, arms open . . . beckoning to her. *I'm going the wrong way.*

She saw a crimson glow surrounding Logan's face.

And then there was nothing.

Chapter Seven

KIRA AWOKE SHIVERING, her back pressed against a hard, unyielding wall, her butt planted on cold, damp concrete. She coughed and rolled her neck, so stiff that pain shot up into her skull with hard, icy fingers.

She glanced around at a world of gray. Everything was neutral and dull . . . the concrete that she sat upon, the brick wall at her back . . . the mist that rolled along the ground.

A groan escaped as she rested her head and ran her tongue along her lips. They felt swollen and burned something fierce.

Shivers racked her body—she was drenched from head to toe. Slowly she unwrapped her arms from around her knees and stood, though she teetered a bit until she gained her balance. Kira's legs felt like spaghetti and her arms had no strength.

Her hair hung in long cords of tangled ebony, well

past her shoulders, and water dripped from the ends to form little pools at her feet. The dress she wore was a tattered ruin. The skirt was ripped from hem to hip and the beautiful shade of yellow had seeped from the fabric.

Like everything else in this place she'd found herself, it was devoid of color. She glanced around and exhaled.

It was devoid of life.

Overhead the crimson moon still shone, but here, tucked in an alley between two buildings, it was muted. Large bins lined the wall to her left—a few of them were overflowing with garbage—and she grimaced at the sight of rats scurrying among them.

Her breath hung in the air as she inched forward until she reached the edge of the alley. Carefully, Kira poked her head out, curious and afraid of what she'd find.

The street in front of her, while deserted, was not painted with the same dull brush as the alley. It was alive with color and scent . . . baked goods and . . . her brow furled . . . caramel candy apples.

Several small cafés lined the street with round tables set up on the sidewalk in front. Red and white checkered cloths covered them, and each boasted a beautiful flower arrangement. A bucket of ice sat there as well, chilling a bottle of wine. Kira had no clue what kind of flowers they were, but the large orange petals were beautiful. A bakery, pub, and a store that sold cheese were also across the way.

Lighting from lampposts along the sidewalk was muted, casting a warm golden glow over the cobblestone road. It took some of the edge off the darker, reddish light from above.

The small street looked like something you'd find in a quaint, European city . . . Paris or Italy. She'd visited Paris once with her parents when she was eight . . . At least she thought she had.

Kira spied a clothing store two doors down from the bakery. The window displayed colorful pieces: a hot pink jacket, a white halter dress, and fuchsia stilettos. When she was sure there was no one around, Kira darted across the street and wove around the many tables set for dinner. She paused in front of Le Grand Design.

The light from the closest lamppost illuminated both the street and the sidewalk. She stared in surprise at her reflection. Slowly her hand reached out and she traced the outline of her face in wonder.

I look like my mother. Hysterical laughter bubbled inside. Who knew?

She flinched as the memory of another reflection and another time rifled through her mind like a shot from a cannon. Pinched features—short, dull, bleached hair and haunted eyes—stared back at her.

Kira blinked and it was gone as fast as it had come, leaving her more than a little rattled. Exhaling, she tried the door and surprisingly—or not—it was unlocked.

Once inside, she closed it behind her, wincing as the latch clicked and echoed into the darkened store. She held her breath but no one came, then slowly released the door as she made her way into the shop.

Racks of clothing surrounded her. Silks, satins, linens in a rainbow of exotic colors. She'd never seen such luxury, and a tentative smile crossed her face as she fingered a dress that fell to the floor in deep plum swaths of silk. She let the cascade slide through her hands and moved on.

Pretty, yes, but not very practical.

She searched through the racks, a shivering mess of wet hair and damp skin, and after a few moments found a t-shirt, stretchy black jeans, and a pair of boots that she could run in.

She grabbed clean underclothes and walked to the back of the store, secure in the shadows that blanketed the corners.

Teeth chattering, Kira set the clothes aside and peeled the wet dress from her body. She dropped it to the floor and stood naked, shivering in the dark. Her thick hair still dripped so she grabbed a scarf from a bin close by and used it to towel-dry the ends, fingers deftly removing what tangles that she could. When she was done she rubbed the rough material down her body—arms, stomach, and legs—until her skin was dry.

A mirror hung on the wall to her right—had it been there before? Slowly she stepped forward and studied herself in its reflection, her hands caressing flesh that was flush with health.

Her breasts were full, no bruises were visible, and—she held her hands in front of her—the scars were still gone. This was the perfect reflection of what she'd always wanted to be.

Of what she could have been.

A wave of sadness rolled over Kira. She didn't understand any of this. Was she really dead? How could she be when, truthfully, she'd never felt so alive?

She wiped away a tear that stung the corner of her eye and froze as goose bumps spread along her flesh like fire across the plains. Glancing up, she peered into the mirror and the world faded away. For what seemed like minutes but had to have only been a few seconds, her gaze was caught by the man behind her.

Logan's eyes, dark as oil, liquefied and slowly changed color until they burned through the gloom like twin points of crimson fire.

"Where did you . . . how did you . . ." she began breathlessly, but the look in his eyes silenced her. His dark hair was slicked back and his clothes clung to him, like a wet second skin. The man sported more than a six-pack and she could see every single one of his abs.

He was hard. Unyielding.

He moved closer and the heat from his body caressed her flesh with an intimate brush that left her trembling. Kira couldn't look away if she wanted to.

When he was near everything was off kilter. Down was up. Back was front. Dark was light. There was something primal about Logan that scared the crap out of her, and yet, for whatever reason, she was drawn to him.

He was the beast—the harbinger of her nightmares—but he was also the man who'd brought her back from that dark place. The man who'd saved her less than an hour ago.

He was the only thing that seemed real in this place.

His eyes burned through the mirror and he did a slow perusal, traveling the length of her—lingering on her breasts even as her hands drew up to cover them—and sweeping down to the juncture between her legs.

Kira's cheeks burned red, hot with humiliation. Her body trembled and for a moment she didn't know what to do. She'd never been naked with a man before . . . not like this. Mergerone, his hands and crazed eyes, didn't count. Confusion didn't come close to describing the thoughts that flew around inside her head.

His eyes narrowed and she didn't like the sly grin that spread across his face as he leaned in even closer—so close that his scent wafted in the air, filling her nostrils. He was all male, full of spice, musk . . . sweat and danger.

Kira's hands were frozen in midair—she wanted to cover herself, but she paused instead and shoved her chin up. She wouldn't give him the pleasure of knowing he'd gotten under her skin.

"A real gentleman would turn around."

His teeth flashed white as his smile widened, though his eyes remained hard as stone. "Lady, there's nothing gentle about me, and as you now know, I'm no *man,* either."

"No shit," she muttered under her breath.

"And as much as I appreciate the peep show, I'd get into some clothes if I were you."

Her eyes flashed steel blue as she met his gaze full-on. "What? Don't think you can control yourself around me?"

"Control isn't the issue." His smile vanished and the flame that lit his eyes intensified. "This isn't a game, little girl." She swallowed heavily at his low growl. "And it's not me you should be worried about."

Logan nodded toward the store window and Kira's stomach clenched so tight she thought she was going to be sick. Hundreds of the same creatures that had come after them in the park lined the sidewalk opposite Le Grand Design. *Hundreds*. They stood shoulder to shoulder and stared toward the store in silence.

The red moon had disappeared and rain now fell, great big drops of it that splattered up inches upon hitting the pavement. The alley behind them, the other storefronts— all of it had disappeared. There were only the trojans. It was truly a sobering sight. Gray mist mingled with shadows and light that slithered across their powerful forms. Massive heads with dark, silent eyes looked as if they could stare into her soul.

"Shit," she whispered.

Logan ignored her, scooped her clothes off the floor, and tossed them at her none too gently. He turned around and she supposed she should be grateful for that, but she caught sight of the muscle that worked its way across his cheek, the tight set to his mouth.

That spelled worry and that scared her more than anything.

Trying to ignore the painful tightness in her chest, she dragged the jeans up over her hips and pulled the t-shirt over her head. Next she slipped her feet into the boots and straightened up, her gaze settled on the crowd outside.

"What are they waiting for?"

A long moment passed before he answered, his rough voice loud in the quiet.

"They're done waiting. The master has arrived."

Chapter Eight

LOGAN'S SHOULDER HURT like a son of a bitch. He cracked his neck and put the pain aside. One of the trojans had latched on but good before he'd had a chance to snap the bastard's neck.

He glanced outside once more and frowned. A sore shoulder was the least of his worries.

"You dressed?" Creamy flesh; soft, feminine lines; and long bits of hair flashed before his eyes. He shook his head aggressively. No fucking time for that either.

"Yes."

Kira moved beside him—she barely reached his shoulders, though the determined chin and squared shoulders made her seem taller somehow.

He knew it was a front . . . her fear hung in the air like a wet towel, its scent cloying and thick. For the hundredth time he cursed Askelon—or Bill, as the little fucker wanted to be called. This mission was a hopeless mess and at the moment he had no idea how he was going to get both himself and Kira to safety.

Time was ticking and he knew his window of opportunity was fast leaving.

Logan whirled around. "Where's the exit?"

Kira ran to the door and swung the deadbolt into place. He arched a brow. If the girl thought that would stop the mass of trojans she was sadly mistaken.

"I don't . . . I don't think there's another door."

His gaze moved over the entire room and he realized she was right. There was no door, no changing rooms. Nothing.

A loud moaning rent the air and his beast shifted once again, the pull painful as fire ripped across his shoulder. The trojans were restless, waiting for the command from their master. As of yet, Logan couldn't see the fucker, but he sure as hell smelled him.

It was the traitor. The one who'd ended Kira's life in the human realm, and Logan still had no idea who it was. If not for the human, he'd sure as hell find out. But he couldn't chance anything. Her life was on the line and she was much too fragile.

"There has to be another way out of here. You need to think and do it fast." He motioned around the store. "All of this means something to you. That is what the gray realm does. It brings to life bits and pieces of your soul . . . of your memories."

She shook her head, not understanding.

"You've been here before." He stepped toward her. "Think!"

The keening noises from outside grew louder. "They're not gonna take a smoke break while you dive through the mess that is your mind."

"You're an asshole."

"Old news."

She tugged a long piece of hair from her eyes and whirled around. She was completely still for a moment and Logan's anger reached near boiling. He'd do whatever it took to get her out of the gray realm, and then he was going to find Bill and kick his sorry little ass all over the fucking place.

"There!" She ran behind the counter that held the cash register and disappeared from his sight. "You were right. I was here when I was, like, eight or something, with my mother. It's a shop in Paris."

Logan reached her just as she drew back the carpeting behind the counter and grinned up at him to reveal a trap door. "When I was here with mother there was an attempted robbery, I think, or something." Her brows furled and fear replaced the excitement. "Someone was after me . . . a man." She glanced up at him. "His face wasn't real. It kept changing."

Sounded otherworld to him.

She shook her head. "I don't understand, but I remember the clerk sending us down here."

Logan grabbed the edge of the trap door and ripped it back. Dank, stale air rose up and he didn't bother to look down. What was the point? He nodded into the darkness.

"You ready for this?"

"Hell, no." She tossed a quick smile his way and he

watched, surprised, as Kira jumped down. Logan followed suit and tugged the heavy door behind him.

He landed in ice-cold water and it took a bit for his eyes to adjust. His nostrils were full of Kira, of old, dead air, and wet cement. A heavy rumbling was heard and the foundation began to vibrate. It was subtle at first but within seconds they were both struggling to keep their balance.

Logan's eyes, now well adjusted, bored into Kira's. "We've no time." He pointed to his right. "That way. I'll follow."

Her eyes were wide and though he smelled fear, he saw determination. She nodded—a quick, curt move—and took off at a good run.

They were in an underground sewer system and their breath misted into clouds that disappeared almost immediately. The walls were rounded—dark gray wet cement—and the pipes that ran overhead glowed an eerie green color. None of this made sense, but Logan had learned long ago that not much in either the lower or upper realms ever did.

The gray realm was a total mind fuck. All of this was part of Kira's past, and even though he knew she wasn't technically crazy, she wasn't untouched either. She was part of the otherworld, whether she liked it or not.

An unearthly screech sounded somewhere behind them and Kira stumbled, this time the fear evident as she glanced behind them.

"They're here, in the tunnel."

"Down there." Logan pushed her to the left, down a narrow shaft. He knew they couldn't outrun the bastards. Not like this.

"I don't . . . Logan, where can we go?"

Her hand was on his chest, the only warmth to be found. He stared down at her for several seconds, watched as her eyes widened, filled with something else. Awareness?

"The only way we can outrun them is if I shift." He waited for a heartbeat. "I know you're scared of what I am, but you'll have to trust that I won't hurt you."

Her hand slowly slipped away and he was surprised at the strong urge he felt to grab it, to hold it against him and drink in her warmth and softness.

Logan backed away, his gaze not leaving hers, and when he thought she was ready . . . when the noise from down the sewer grew louder . . . he called on the ancient magick of his people.

His human clothes slipped away, disappearing into the nothing as mist rolled over his body. Limbs elongated and cracked—painfully—but it was something he relished—the pain. It spoke of his power and of his heritage and of the beast that lived inside him. As his body size tripled and quadrupled, never once did his gaze falter.

Kira's face was pale, her mouth pinched, but she didn't move an inch as he stood before her, a hellhound. Her fear had tripled and how could it not? He was the size of large horse.

The rumble of hundreds of trojans shook the foundation of the sewer. He bared his teeth and shook his head, stretching his long legs in front of him so that she would be able to climb on.

Her hands, tentative at first, sank slowly into the thick fur between his shoulder blades, but then she dug in with her fists and hopped on top of him. She slid forward and her arms wrapped themselves around his neck, her legs pinned tight to his ribs.

"Get me out of here," she whispered hoarsely, "please."

Logan took off. His long legs and preternatural speed carried them down the shaft in a blur of fur, fangs, and Kira. His nostrils flared as hundreds of scents flew at him. When he was in his hellhound form all of his abilities were amplified. He became the ultimate tracker, and once he was set on a scent there was no escaping.

He twisted and turned, going left and then right, picking up speed as adrenaline flooded his cells. After a while there was only the sound of water splashing against his paws, of his heart beating heavy in his chest, and of the ragged breaths falling from Kira.

He didn't slow down—if anything, he picked up speed and held his head low as he streaked through the underground tunnels wanting to put as much distance between him and the trojans.

Eventually the dank smell of the sewer lessened and his ears pricked forward as he was able to filter other sounds.

A crowd. Laughter. Excitement.

By Logan's estimation he'd been running for nearly an hour. He had no idea what was above them, but it was time to find out. The clock was ticking. He needed to get Kira back to the Regent Institute before her human form degenerated.

He came to a stop and waited for her to slip from atop his body before he called upon his human skin. He transitioned as fast as he could, welcoming the pain—anything to distract him from the conflicting emotions Kira brought out in him. Moments later he stood before her, staring at her in silence. The eerie glow from pipes above them danced off the water and encircled her in swaths of green light.

Her hair was a mess of tangles, her eyes large, luminous balls of oil. Her mouth parted and he saw the tip of her tongue. She took a step toward him, unsure, her tongue now moistening her lips as she bit down.

For a second he imagined that tongue wet and glistening, gliding across something else. Logan exhaled harshly, banishing the image from his mind just as quick. What the hell was wrong with him?

"That was . . ." She ran shaking hands through the tangles at her neck. "That was incredible. You're incredible. I've never . . ."

"Christ. If I had a dollar for every time I've heard that line, I'd be a fucking millionaire." The result was worth it.

Her lips pinched briefly, and the fire he needed to see in her eyes returned. Considering what lay ahead, she sure as hell was going to need it.

Kira rested her hands on her hips and the tongue that had been teasing him disappeared, which, if he was to be honest, was disappointing.

"You may be an incredible . . . dog or whatever the hell you—"

"Wrong."

"What?"

"A dog is a pet."

"And?" Her brow was arched as she took a step closer.

"I'm no pet."

"So what are you, then? A big-ass fur ball with fangs?" She was pissed now.

Logan's eyes glowed red as he leaned down until only a whisper separated his mouth from hers. "I'm like nothing you've ever met before, lady."

"You got that right." She retorted. She pushed him away and took a step back. "My entire world has been the Institute and crazy people. *Real crazy people.*" Her chest was heaving with anger. "Nurses with syringes, orderlies, and doctors." She was nearly spitting at him now. "Mergerone with his lectures, and greasy smile, and hands and . . ."

"And what?" His voice was sharp. He sensed her pain.

Kira smoothed her hair and exhaled. "Nothing." She whirled around and jumped on the steel ladder that led topside. "What do you care? It's all your fault anyway. You invaded my life when I was ten and I've been in hell ever since."

Logan watched her scramble for the surface, his jaw clenched tight, his brows furled. She thought she knew what hell was? Kira Dove had no fucking clue.

Logan grabbed the bottom rung and quickly followed her up. If he was lucky, he might be able to save her from finding out.

Chapter Nine

KIRA KNEW THAT Logan was right behind her, but even so, she tensed when his long arms reached around and pushed the sewer grate open. She scrambled out and immediately rolled to the side as two large wooden stilts crashed down around her.

Noise flooded her ears. Laughter, songs, conversations. It was a mad melee of music and people.

Strong arms lifted her and Kira blinked rapidly, rubbing her eyes as the darkness gave way to a bright sun and a kaleidoscope of color. From atop stilts, a pale man in red, white, and blue—sporting an Uncle Sam beard and hat—grinned down at her.

She had no time at all to wonder, to look and to take in—Logan had her hand gripped firmly inside his and pulled her through a crowd that danced and sang.

"Stay close and keep your head low." Logan said

tersely, his breath warm against her ear. "Those that don't belong are watching."

They were in the middle of a parade of sorts, a mad crush of people running through the streets waving banners that made no sense—symbols with markings beneath them—she didn't understand any of the words.

The sidewalks were filled with folk as well, watching and cheering as the group in the street passed. They were as varied in dress as those who surrounded Kira—similar to what she'd seen in the market. Men, women, and children were draped in silks and satins, cotton, denim, and leather. Kira spotted a nun and Sumo wrestler. All were laughing, enjoying whatever it was Kira and Logan were now part of.

But somehow it didn't ring true, as if the music notes on first listen, though perfect, were off key.

Kira caught the eye of a tall, thin man who nodded as she passed. His complexion was as pale as his dirty gray shirt and pocked with many scars that gave him a craggy appearance. He wore a dark pinstripe suit and shiny patent leather shoes, and sported a dingy fedora that at one time must have been black, but now was faded to a dull gray.

Oh God, how she hated gray.

He touched the brim of his hat and smiled, his dark eyes glowing a vibrant green for just a second. His teeth were yellowed, his tongue black, and she was fairly certain maggots twisted and turned along the corners of his mouth.

Kira couldn't tear her eyes away, even though the sight of him made her stomach roil.

Logan tugged on her hand, murmuring, "This way," and she was forced to follow as they wove among the crowd. Kira chanced a look back and swallowed thickly as maggot man's gaze continued to follow them. His smile widened and the queasiness inside her belly tripled.

Her hand gripped Logan's tightly and he paused, his eyes as dark as obsidian. "Are you all right?"

Was that concern in his voice?

Her cheeks flushed, her heart sped up. He was so big that she had to crank her neck back in order to meet his gaze. She shook her head—didn't trust her voice to speak so she remained silent.

"You need to suck it up and grow a set. Contrary to what you may believe, this isn't all about you. My ass is on the line, too, and I don't mean to get it shot to hell here in this place."

Concern? Hell, no. The only thing he cared about was himself.

"Let's go."

They swept along with the crowd and she took a few moments to study the street. Logan had said this "gray realm," as he called it, held memories from her mind. Of course that didn't make any sense to her, but she was willing to go along with it since it seemed to be true, judging from the market and Central Park.

They were on a main street of a small, picture-perfect town. The storefronts were quaint, whitewashed with blue trim. All of them. They boasted intricate wood design along the roofs, painted in crisp white trim, very much like a gingerbread house. Overhead seagulls flew, and as her eyes followed a pair of them, she smelled the scent of the ocean.

Sand, sea, and salt.

One of the signs hanging above a store caught her eye: The Sea Shell. It triggered pictures, memories of lazy summer afternoons at the beach, ice cream, and summer's end carnivals.

"I know this place," she whispered. *My family has a summer house close by on the beach.*

The crowd spilled into a large field that boasted rides and games for everyone. Kira smiled at the sight of a massive red, white, and blue Ferris wheel. It lumbered slowly, turning in a circle as the off-key song continued to play.

Booths filled to the brim with stuffed animals and candy and prizes galore greeted her. It was overwhelming. The smell, sounds, and crush of people.

A rush of gold and white appeared among the crowd—it was the dog she'd seen in the market—followed by the little boy. The young child laughed loudly as he followed the barking animal, waving his hands above his head like an airplane. He ran past, his mouth alive with buzzing noises as he snaked crazily through the crowd.

Logan swore as she dug in her heels so that she could watch him, and when the boy reached the Ferris wheel, he stopped and turned back to her. Their eyes locked and the smile disappeared from his face.

A chill swept over Kira. Was the child trying to tell her something?

"I told you to keep your head down, Dove. What part of that don't you understand?" Logan's anger snapped her out of it. She blinked, but when she looked again, the boy was gone.

Kira yanked her hand from his. "I don't understand any of this." She stepped back—chest tight, heart pounding hard and heavy inside her—and turned in a circle. She winced as she caught sight of yellow-tooth maggot-mouth man. He was following her.

Logan's hand was on her shoulder and he spun her around. He was close. His scent was inside her. His spice, his overwhelming maleness . . . his strength. He was a man and an animal. On what planet was that even possible?

His mouth was tight and she knew he was angry. Well, too fucking bad—so was she. Kira had had enough.

"I want answers now." She took a step backward.

He growled, "Kira—"

"No," she interrupted. "No, no, no! I don't want to hear 'Kira.' I don't want to hear anything but the goddamn truth."

His face darkened into a cold mask and his chest rumbled as he stared back at her.

"And I *really* don't want to hear that either."

"That?" he said stiffly.

She thumped him on the chest. "That animal sound you make or whatever the heck it is." She snorted. "It's not normal. None of this is normal or right or even possible. I'm not going anywhere with you until I know exactly what happened to me fifteen years ago."

Logan swore and tried to grab her, but she stepped

back and twisted out of his reach. His eyes flashed blood red and she knew his anger had just ramped up big time.

"You stupid little girl. You have no idea what the hell is going on because if you did—"

"Enlighten me, asshole."

Logan's face whitened. He stared at her for several moments, eyes cold and harsh.

"Before this is all over, you will pay for your insolence—understand?"

No, I don't.

Kira leaned ·forward, as if she was about to share a confidence, and whispered. "Fuck you."

She'd crossed a line . . . hell, she'd damn well jumped over it, but in that moment it felt more like she'd just reclaimed something.

Her life.

She whirled around and rushed into the crowd, ignoring his bark of rage. She was filled with a shot of exhilaration, or maybe it was adrenaline or something else entirely. Whatever it was, she liked it.

The trojans and the terror she'd felt in the sewer disappeared as the carnival-like atmosphere surrounded her. She wanted to lose herself in it and never come back.

"Dove, get your ass back here." His voice had elevated from pissed off to pure rage.

She ignored him, accepted a huge pink balloon of cotton candy as she ran past a six-foot clown. It was reckless what she was doing, but it felt sweeter than the pink cloud of sugar in her hands.

Kira darted among the crowd, her legs strong and sure as she slipped around the people, running past the rides, the games, and food booths. Ahead she saw the dog—the small golden thing from before—waving its tail rapidly, its little chest heaving as it barked crazily . . . at her.

She ran toward the animal, wincing at the bellow that followed behind her. All of a sudden everything seemed much more in her face. The crowd was louder and a hint of menace touched all of them, electrifying the air and filling her chest with dread.

The dog disappeared between something called The Zipper and a red-and-white–striped candy apple stand. Kira stayed hot on its heels, though she stopped abruptly when she rounded the side of the tall ride. Thick, rolling mist swirled in front of her—a wall of it—and everything around her was flooded with its heaviness. The sounds of the carnival faded as the wet air slid over her.

A touch of fear turned in her gut. It was as if the carnival had never existed. She stumbled, blind as a bat, until finally the fog cleared and she found herself in the middle of the market.

A cool breeze swept along the street, spreading bits of paper and refuse into the air. They danced like snowflakes, hitting her in the face and arms. The sun was hiding, the colors and scents of the Caribbean gone—not a soul stirred and Catherine's booth was empty.

The entire market was painted by the same dull gray brush that seemed to follow her everywhere.

"If I never see this color again . . ." Kira muttered.

She stepped forward and winced at the sad echo of

her boots on the pavement. Her gaze darted here and there, searching for anyone who might be hiding in the shadows, but there was no one. A bark echoed from down the way and Kira peered into the gloom. Suddenly the wisdom of following the dog was definitely in doubt.

"Shit," she murmured, unsure and feeling very much alone. She heard a scuff behind her and froze.

"You are the most annoying, frustrating, and ill-behaved human I've ever met."

It was Logan. She relaxed a bit and turned around. He stood a few inches from her, hands fisted at his sides and mouth set into a tight, grim line.

"Human? You say that like it's a disease or something. Should I be insulted?"

A vein throbbed near his temple. "This isn't a fucking game."

"Really? What is it? 'Cause I have no idea. No one's had the balls to let me in on that little secret."

His dark eyes studied her in silence and she shifted, uncomfortable beneath his intense glare. "I don't have time for this."

"Newsflash, buddy. If I'm already dead, then seems to me I should have all the time in the world."

He snarled as he moved closer, and though Kira would have preferred to keep some space between them, she refused to budge. "That's where you're wrong, little girl."

"Don't call me little girl." She spat at him.

"Then stop acting like one. Your situation is a lot more serious than it appears, and right now death is the least of your worries."

"I find that hard to believe." But Kira saw the look in his eyes and her stomach twisted harder than it already was.

Logan ignored her. "Time is your enemy." He paused, ran his hands through his hair, and nailed her with a look that spoke volumes. "The clock is ticking and you're almost out of it."

Chapter Ten

THE DOG SHE'D been following howled. It was a hair-splitting cry that cut between the two of them and ended on an abrupt note that was jarring. Silence followed, the kind that weighed heavily. Fear, thick and foul tasting, filled Kira's mouth, and when Logan grabbed her hand she offered no resistance.

His touch wasn't gentle—in fact, his fingers dug into her flesh, causing her to wince. But it was real, and hard, and if she knew nothing at all, she knew that blood flowed beneath his veins the same as hers. And in this place of chaos and falsehood, it was reassuring.

They ran across the deserted street and headed toward a series of buildings that bordered two of the four sides of the market square. What made up the remainder of the square couldn't be seen; the fog was too thick. Logan pushed open the third door and bolted it behind them once they were inside. Only then did he let go of her hand.

They were in some kind of gift shop, one filled with candles, pottery, and artwork. Several large and small canvases filled the walls, full of varying shades of gray with the odd dash of color. Kira glanced at them but they didn't register, not really. Nothing in here did. She couldn't focus.

You're almost out of time.

That's what Logan had said. But what did he mean?

She turned to him and was more than a little unnerved to find his dark eyes settled onto her, arms crossed over his chest as he glared at her.

"I want some answers or . . . I'm not going anywhere with you." Did she sound childish? Maybe. Did she give a rat's ass? Hell, no.

He remained silent and anger stirred within Kira. "Who are you?" She shook her head savagely. "No, that's wrong. I think the question should be *what* are you."

"Hellhound."

"Say again?"

Logan moved toward the window and peered out. He dropped the blinds and turned back to her. It was several degrees darker now, and the shadows that flickered across his face made him look a hundred times fiercer than he already was.

"I'm a hellhound. I *escort* souls to the hell realm for processing."

"Hellhound," she repeated as an image of his furriness flashed before her eyes. She thought that maybe a normal person would reject what he'd just shared. But how could she? After all she'd seen?

"Are we talking . . ." She pointed below and waited, breath caught in her throat as he nodded. *Okay, then.*

"I'm not sure I understand exactly," she paused, "what you mean."

"Souls that have been marked for the lower realm usually require," a ghost of a smile played around his mouth, though his eyes remained cold as winter, "a little coaxing." He shrugged. "Most try to escape, but once scented, there is no evading a hellhound. I bring them in to be processed."

"Processed?"

Logan was quiet for a moment. "I guess 'sentenced' would be the correct word."

She snorted. "You have a judge and jury in hell?"

He shook his head. "No judge. No jury. Just a pissed off demon who decides what district the term will be served in. District One being almost heavenly compared to, say, District Three." Logan's smile was harsh. "Trust me. Rarely does one get sentenced to District One for the term of their punishment."

"Term?"

He shrugged. "Term means nothing, really. A trip below means forever. Once you've been marked, there is no turning back." Logan watched her closely. "Hell is no different from anyplace else. There is order," he grimaced, "of a sort."

Kira's mind moved fast, processing what Logan had shared. "So, when I was ten you came for me because I'd been marked?"

He nodded but remained silent.

Flashes of heat, moans of pain, and the smell of fear as

thick as acrid smoke filled her mind. She exhaled slowly and took a few steps, needing some space between them.

His dark eyes followed her as she moved away—she felt them on her skin as surely as if he'd taken his hands and run them across her shoulders and down her arms. A shiver followed in their wake and she ran fingers through the tangles that fell around her face.

Why?

"I was ordered to."

Okay, he was a mind reader now?

"Ordered . . . you have a boss?"

"I answer to the Overlord Santos."

"Overlord," she repeated. "That makes sense." Her eyes flashed. "It's not like you'd have a boss called, say . . . Mr. Smith or Mrs. Hannigan or anything like that. No way, because that would be *normal* and you're about as far away from," she felt him just behind her and froze, "normal as you can get." She finished in a whisper.

"We don't have time for this, Kira."

The way he said her name made her feel hot inside and more than a little shaky. She couldn't let him rattle her. Not now. She needed the truth.

"You told me I was dead. I don't get that." Kira whirled around and ate the squeal that sat at the back of her throat. He was much too close. Much too large . . . and much too male.

"In the human realm, your body lies in a morgue at the Regent Institute."

"The human realm," she repeated. Right. Because this was so not the human realm.

Light flashed inside her head as pain lanced across her skull. She groaned and doubled over, hating the pictures that ran through her mind. Mergerone. His hands. His face and smell. The new orderlies. Their glee at her pain and their relentless attack.

"No," she whispered in horror as she backed away. Fists pounding against flesh rang in her ears and a sob escaped from between her lips. "I tried," she whispered. "I knew they wouldn't let me leave that room alive. They were too big and too strong and they . . ." Her eyes sought out Logan's. "They weren't human and there was . . ."

"Go on," he prompted, his voice as gentle as it was going to get.

"There was someone in the shadows. I couldn't see his face but I *felt* him. Felt his sadistic joy." She let out a shuddering breath. "Why? Why would they want to kill me . . . ?" Her voice trailed into nothing as she stared at him.

Logan moved closer yet, and this time she welcomed the energy and strength that he gave off. Kira watched the steady rise and fall of his chest. She inhaled the earthy, exotic scent of him, and for one brief moment wanted nothing more than to move into his arms and forget everything.

"I can't answer your questions."

Of course.

Kira had never felt so alone. "Can't or won't?" she said bitterly.

"Both" was his curt reply. "I need to get you out of here alive and take you back."

"Take me back? Where? To your so-called *human*

realm? But if I'm dead, then what?" She shook her head. "I don't understand."

His eyes narrowed. "You don't need to understand." He leaned forward. "You need to listen."

The dog began to bark once more.

Kira exhaled stiffly and tore her eyes away from his. He made her nervous. The man was much too intense and held too many secrets.

Could this be one of her nightmares? It seemed plausible. She rubbed her temple and winced as the beginnings of a headache erupted. There was no alternative but to go with it and see where she ended up. Was she alive? Dead? Or somewhere in between?

"Okay." She pulled away. "What's the plan?"

"We find the portal."

"Portal?" This was the stuff of science fiction novels.

"Do you remember where you were when you first arrived here?"

"No, not really." Kira shook her head but then she paused. "I think I was here in the market." Her brow furled. "No, no, that's wrong . . . hold on." The pressure inside her head was incredible, pressing behind her optic nerves with a ferocity that left her dizzy. Blotches of color, the sensation of soft cotton sheets and floating on air surrounded her. It was blurry at first, then like water receding in the tide, the mist cleared. "My first memory of this place was at my house. I was in my bedroom in Beverly Hills."

"Do you remember where the house was in relation to this market?"

"No." Panic set in and she began to pace.

"Do you remember any sounds or maybe a smell? The gray realm is constantly shifting but smells linger and we might get lucky."

A thought crossed her mind. "How did you get here?"

"That path is closed."

"Why?"

"Let's just say I don't bring out the warm fuzzies in the gatekeeper." His eyes narrowed, his voice was firm. "Tick tock, tick tock . . . I need you to remember."

Kira cracked her neck and tried to ease the tension that lay across her shoulders. It was no use. She was strung tighter than a bow around an arrow. Still, she closed her eyes and concentrated. Nothing but a blank canvas came to mind. "It hurts," she whispered.

"Try harder." There was no compassion in his voice, but did she really expect it?

The dog's barking had reached a level that signaled the game had changed—at this very moment the trojans might have arrived with their master close at hand. Yet Kira shut it out, covering her ears with her hands as she searched her mind. Pain sliced through her skull and she cried out.

Then, like a leak that had been sprung, a small crack appeared in her memories. It fingered out—thin spidery legs of images, smells, and sensations. She turned to Logan and whispered, "French toast."

"French toast," he repeated, watching her closely.

She nodded. "Someone brought me breakfast. It was there beside my bed. French toast, maple syrup, and scrambled eggs." Her brow furled. "I reached for the plate." Eyes wide, she stared up into his. "It had been so long since I'd had anything like it, but . . ." she exhaled. "It disappeared . . . right before my eyes. When I rolled out of bed everything went weird, like the floor was mushy and the walls changed color. I was off balance and the next thing I remember is standing at the edge of the market."

"French toast," he murmured. Blue eyes stared into dark ones. "You did good, kid." He nodded toward the back of the shop. "This way."

Kira's gaze rested on his broad shoulders, her face flushed at the small crumb of praise. He opened the door and glanced back at her, hand beckoning toward the swirling mist beyond. His nostrils flared and his eyes sparked crimson.

Most people would run the other way at the sight of such a man. He was too large, too intimidating . . . too much an alpha male. And then there was the whole turning-into-an-animal thing.

This man or hellhound—or whatever he was—held her life in the palm of his hand. He was asking her to believe in things that were beyond believable for most people, and yet . . . she trusted him completely.

Which made no sense.

"Nothing about this makes sense," she said under her breath.

Kira started forward, a prayer on her lips as she slipped past Logan and disappeared into the heavy mist. It was the first prayer she'd uttered in over fifteen years.

She just hoped someone was listening.

Chapter Eleven

THE SMELLS OUT here were sharp. They tingled along the inside of Logan's nose and he filtered out the ones he wanted before moving forward. His long legs ate up the concrete while Kira's smaller ones pumped fast in order to keep up with him. He supposed he could slow down—match his strides with hers—but the need to complete the mission tore at him.

The gray realm made him edgy. Kira made him edgy. And that left the bad taste of losing control in his mouth. Something he didn't much care for.

He glanced down at her. She was surprising to him . . . for a human, and that was saying something. They were a race of beings he'd always thought of as weak, and he'd never much cared for them. Not the way Bill did. He had to wonder what it was about Kira that made her of special interest for those of the otherworld. Especially the one who was here, tracking her in the gray realm.

His mouth tightened at the thought of the faceless assassin. Damn, but he'd love a chance at his ass—how cowardly to stalk a human girl with no chance of protecting herself. Logan snarled and clenched his hands. He might get a chance yet.

He hazarded a glance behind them but wasn't able to penetrate through the fog that swirled ever faster. At the moment it seemed they were alone.

He'd found the smallest thread of a scent that could be what he was looking for. French toast? Who knew, but it was sweet—sickeningly so—and more importantly, it was linked to Kira's scent, which carried bits of sun and soul.

Logan grabbed her hand and guided her to the right. The wind picked up—slicing through the mist and thinning it—as it swept along the ground in turbulent gusts. At his feet the concrete suddenly gave way to soft grass, his heavy boots sinking into its softness, and he sniffed—water was nearby.

One second they were rushing through gray; the next, they were nearly blinded by sunlight.

Logan pulled up at the sight before him—an opulent house faced with delicate pink stucco and white trim, a sea of green and blue, and a riot of color everywhere else.

Kira trembled in his grasp and he watched as her face came alive. Her eyes widened—their recesses shiny, now reflective pools of onyx—and her generous mouth curved into a soft smile. For a few seconds she appeared much younger, as if no worry lived inside her soul. Long hair wafted about her face, and he reached for a tendril that floated behind her ear but stopped short of touching it.

What the hell was he doing?

He cleared his throat and extricated his hand from hers. She didn't seem to notice, and he followed as she began to jog and then run toward the pool.

This backyard oasis was alive with color. No gray existed here. Gardens fell along the fence, a riot of pinks, oranges, yellows, and purples. Tall, exotic trees lined the border, a fountain with a mermaid shooting water several feet in the air lay to his left—its gray foundation was bordered by the bluest irises he'd ever seen.

Logan snorted at the thought. He supposed most creatures—human or otherworld—would be surprised that he had a bit of a green thumb. Gardening was his therapy. When he'd been imprisoned in the Pit, the one thing he missed most was the garden he kept at his home.

There was something beautiful in the simple organic makeup of plants.

His gaze drifted toward the pool. This was extravagant, even for the well-heeled and moneyed humans who dwelled in Beverly Hills. Several waterfalls dropped buckets of shimmery, fresh liquid—the color of the deepest part of the Caribbean—into the pool. There was a diving board, hot tub off to the right, and to his left an impressive swim-up bar.

"Nana."

Kira's tortured whisper drew his gaze and he started forward with purpose. Time was wasting and there was someone beyond the pool. He couldn't see who it was, but the presence held power.

He reached the patio a second behind Kira, and watched closely as an old woman turned toward them. Her hair was silver and fell past her shoulders in long waves, the face warm and kind—though her eyes were much colder when they landed on Logan.

She was otherworld—the scent was unmistakable—though Logan couldn't quite determine exactly *what* she was.

"Catherine . . . I thought you were Nana." Disappointment rang in Kira's voice and her shoulders slumped slightly as she exhaled a long, shuddering breath.

"No, my dear, she moved on a long time ago." The woman glanced up at Logan and she frowned, her brows drawn tight. "You're guiding her back?"

Logan nodded, well aware of the distaste that sat in the old woman's eyes. He smiled, a fuck-you salute. "Unless you've got someone else who can get the job done."

Her eyes narrowed for a second, but then she ignored him and turned to Kira. "I've been waiting for you, but make no mistake, you're in grave danger. We've got to hurry." The woman glanced behind Logan, her lips tight as she shook her head. "They're not far behind. Follow me."

Logan prodded Kira forward and they disappeared inside after the old woman. The house was as impressive as the outside—humans seemed to love rich, exotic things. And the ones who could afford these rich trappings seemed to have the least amount of taste. The old adage "less is more" sure as hell didn't live in this house.

He ignored all of it and followed Kira and the woman,

Catherine, through a kitchen and up a large, circular stairway that led to a posh upper level.

He knew this home. He'd been in it fifteen years earlier. It was exactly as he remembered.

"Here we are, dear." The woman smoothed wrinkled, worn hands over the long, colorful skirt she wore. Bangles jingled at her wrist, sounding like tinkling water.

Kira stepped forward and hugged the old lady tightly and whispered, "Thank you."

Catherine glanced at Logan and even he was impressed with how fast the warmth fled her eyes. "Take care of her, hound, or I shall haunt you for eternity." She stepped out of Kira's embrace and motioned toward the far end of the landing. "Hurry, hurry."

Logan tapped Kira on the shoulder. "We have to go."

She nodded and pointed toward the far end of the landing. "My room is there."

He knew that, of course, but remained silent as he followed her. She threw open the door and Logan blinked. Shit, he didn't remember it being so . . . nauseatingly girlish. An assault of pink and white greeted him, as if a bag of marshmallows and cotton candy had exploded everywhere.

The door closed behind him and he moved into the room, nostrils flaring as he opened up his senses and scanned the entire perimeter. On a large pedestal base, in the center of the room, was a four-poster bed. White gauzy wisps of fabric fell from the ceiling to touch the floor around it. Off to the right a small white sofa and table were arranged beneath the window. Books and magazines were scattered across the table and a large dollhouse stood nearby.

With eyes closed he visualized Kira's energy, those shimmering threads of her soul, and he followed the wispy strands. They led him to her bedroom closet.

"Well, this is cliché," he murmured. "All right, let's do this." The door opened beneath his fingers, exposing a large walk-in. The energy inside the room pulsed with otherworld magic and he knew the portal was still there. Lucky for them—the damn things had a habit of moving around at will, especially in this realm.

"Let's go, Kira."

Logan glanced back and froze. She stood in front of a floor-to-ceiling mirror—inches from it—her fingers upon her face as she stared at herself. She looked sad, lost. When she looked up suddenly and their eyes met, something twisted inside of Logan. Something hard. It was a physical reaction and the muscles in his gut tightened. What it was he reacted to, he couldn't be sure of. The only thing he did know was that he didn't like it.

Not one bit.

"I don't . . ." Her eyes dropped to the ground, her voice was barely heard. "I don't really look like this." Her shoulders hunched forward. "Not back there." She paused and then looked up, her dark eyes haunting as she stared at him through the mirror. "Not anymore."

Suddenly he understood. "I know." He answered gruffly.

Surprise flickered in her eyes and she turned to him.

"But how would you . . . we've never met. I mean, not as adults."

She ran her tongue along her dry lips. The action drew his eyes and he spent more time than he should have staring at her mouth. Those full lips that were made for sliding and licking and—his groin tightened—all sorts of things he shouldn't be thinking about.

"How do you know what I look like?"

"I tracked you from the morgue."

"The morgue," she repeated, a slight tremor riding her words. "Right." She crossed the room until she stood so close he could touch her. When she looked up at him the sorrow that lay in her eyes punched him in the gut. "I'm dead. So, back there," she blew out a shuddering breath, "back there I'm nothing and after we go back, what are my chances? Am I going to make it?"

The air thickened. Logan was hot and irritated.

Her scent washed over him, the purity of it, and the warmth that was woven into her signature left him tight. His gut churned as he stared down into her dark eyes.

Damn, but he should have tapped that blonde at the bar before Bill had shown. He rolled his shoulders. It had been too long. Now was not the time to be thinking of his dick.

"I'm not going to lie," he said carefully. "I've never brought anyone back from the gray realm, and if we're successful in navigating this portal together," he shrugged, "I have no clue what condition your body is in. Time moves differently here. What seems like a few hours to us might be days in the human realm—or seconds." He shook his head. "It's a total fucking crapshoot."

"I could end up dead, forever dead."

The window was open and the breeze that flew in carried the stink of demon. In the distance the mad barking dog broke through the silence and Logan knew their time was up. The trojans weren't far behind.

"Little Dove, you're already dead. If you stay here you'll end up much worse." He nodded outside. "Whatever is out there will end you, understand? You will cease to exist. At least if we return, you have some kind of chance."

He tried to ignore the big dark eyes that stared up at him, full of worry and anger and something he couldn't quite put his finger on.

He ran his fingers through his damp hair that curled around his neck. Shit, it was hot in here. Logan turned toward the closet. "We gotta roll."

Yet her hand at his back stopped him cold. "Wait."

His skin sizzled where she touched him. Right through his damn shirt. Logan kept his mouth shut as she moved in front of him. He wanted to tell her to back off—to take her hand off him—but he remained silent. Logan Winters wasn't about to lose his cool because a little slip of a human had managed to get under his skin.

Finally she let go and stared up at him, chest heaving and shoulders squared. Her hands clenched into fists at her sides and the knuckles strained white.

"I won't do this until I know . . ." Her voice trailed off and he arched a brow, a muscle working its way across his cheek as the mad barking grew closer. Was he going to have to toss her ass inside?

"Know what?"

She shook her head. "You're going to think I'm crazy." Something in her eyes changed—it wasn't just the slight softening of color from dark chocolate into caramel. It was the emotion behind them, and suddenly he was nervous.

Him. Logan Winters. Hellhound from the fucking land of the damned.

"I've never been kissed before."

Shit, no. We're not going there. And yet his body hardened instantly as if her words plucked him like a cellist pulling her bow.

"I've never made love to anyone." Shadows crept into her face. "He . . . Mergerone raped me." Tears filled the corners of her eyes and she trembled, a sob caught in her throat. "Many times." She whispered. "That's my experience. That's all I've known."

His eyes narrowed and beneath his chest the beast shifted. This Mergerone had touched her. Blind rage colored everything until only a palette of red remained. He would pulverize the bastard. Torture and maim and then kill. Kira was his.

Logan growled. *She was his.*

A roaring echoed in his ears and for a moment reality slid away, leaving only the woman standing before him. Her soul glimmered, surrounding her in a beautiful rainbow of gold. It called to him.

With a savage snarl, Logan shook the image from his head. This was crazy. What the hell was he thinking?

Outside he heard the thunderous boom of feet pounding into the grass and the screeching of birds—and the incessant barking grew louder. It was in the room with them, surrounding them both, and yet it couldn't pierce the wall of emotion Kira had just put out there.

Her gaze was focused on his mouth. He felt her touch as surely as if she was imprinted on his flesh. "If I don't make it, I just want one—"

Logan's groin tightened painfully and he clenched his teeth in order to eat the groan that sat in the back of his throat. Kira needed to shut the hell up and follow him through the portal.

"—kiss," she whispered, placing her hands upon his chest and pulling herself up onto her toes.

The heat of her was everywhere. Her scent was inside his body. He glanced out the large window behind the sitting area, alarmed to see most of the backyard oasis had disappeared as a blanket of gray preceded the onslaught of the trojans. Color was bleeding out of her purgatory as fast as blood seeping from a wound.

They had maybe a minute, most likely less.

Her hand hardened against his jaw, he felt her nails puncture his skin and she pulled him down toward her. He could have resisted, pulled away from her touch, and yet he didn't. Was he fucking crazy?

I want her.

And then her lips were on his, hesitant at first, like a whisper of silk gliding across his mouth. He heard his heart beating fast and furious, felt the tightening of every muscle in his body, and knew he needed to grab her and run.

But desire was a traitorous bitch with no care as to whom she put under her spell. *Just one touch*, he thought, as his large hand sank into the thick hair at her nape. With a groan he pulled her flush against his body and his tongue slid inside her warmth.

Chapter Twelve

THIS WAS MADNESS.

Dimly she was aware of the noise from outside—the dog, the trojans, the thing who wanted her dead—and yet it meant nothing. In this moment—in this room, in this place that existed on another plane entirely—the only thing that mattered was the man who held her.

He was something she'd never had before.

Logan kissed her long and hard, his lips sliding across hers with a boldness that electrified her. His tongue plunged deep and the feel of him inside her mouth drove her crazy. She took from him with aggressive abandon, her tongue stroking, sucking, exploring with equal fervor.

His taste was primal, his scent wholly male, and Kira's head spun. Never in all of her imaginings had she thought it would feel like this. She clung to him like a weakling, as if she would lose herself if she let go.

Her body was hot and cold, heated and wet. The ache

that erupted between her legs was intense—a pounding dance of desire—and she clenched her thighs together, trying to ease the pressure. But it was no use. Her hands dug into him, pulling at his shoulders, wanting to imprint her body along the hard length of him. Her tongue danced along his, tasting and teasing, as they locked together in a passionate embrace that left them both breathless.

Was it the danger? The absolute knowledge that she was about to jump headfirst into an unknown that she might never recover from, that made this so thrilling?

Logan broke away first and she looked up at him, across the harsh light that flickered along his jaw and left half of his face in shadow. His chest heaved and he thrust her away from him, swearing in that freaky language that she didn't understand.

Her hand crept up to her lips, swollen from the passion and fury of his kiss. Every single cell in her body tingled with an awareness that she'd never felt before. It was everything she'd wanted and so much more.

It was the perfect first kiss.

A crash sounded from below, followed by a roar that echoed through the house. The hair on the back of Kira's neck stood on end and her heart nearly jumped into her throat.

"We're out of time." His eyes morphed into deep crimson and she shivered at the furious look that graced their depths. "Move back. I need to shift. It's the only way I can take you through the portal." His voice lowered, the timbre gruff and dangerous. "When I'm ready, grab hold of me and don't let go."

She could only nod.

"It's gonna be tight and there are no guarantees. I hope a kiss was worth it."

Her fingers crept up to touch her lips once more.

Mist crawled along Logan's legs as his clothes disappeared and his body elongated and shifted. Time slowed into long seconds of bones popping, rumbling growls, and eyes that burned red. It was fascinating and horrifying to watch, but Kira was riveted.

Another crash sounded, this time much closer. She swallowed thickly and tried to ignore the lump that sat in her stomach like a stone, as she turned toward the door to her bedroom. It was on its hinges, splinters of wood strewn everywhere, and the large, gaping hole was filled with trojans.

A blinding light emanated from the space between them, flickering along the ceiling in a kaleidoscope of golden rainbows that slowly engulfed the entire room. She blinked and nearly fell over as a large furry head shoved her back toward the closet.

A snarl escaped the hellhound and for one second Kira's gaze was caught and held by Logan's fiery red eyes. He bared his teeth and the rumbling that sounded from his chest was terrifying to hear.

Move back!

Startled, she froze instead, shaking her head at the weird sensation of hearing Logan's voice inside her brain.

But she had no time to process what she was seeing or hearing, for the light spoke. No form fell from inside the shower of gold—there was no person to see. Just a voice.

A disembodied voice that held not an ounce of emotion.

"A dog from the underworld thinks to challenge me?"

Logan's powerful hindquarters shoved her back, deeper into the closet, as he turned to face their attackers. Logan's sides heaved and his long, powerful legs were spread as if ready to pounce.

The trojans shouldered each other restlessly, jockeying for a better position. Their mouths agape, they emitted a sharp hissing sound that hurt Kira's ears. She moved back, her chest tight with fear and the knowledge that this might be her end. Her eyes moved to Logan and a sob caught at the back of her throat. Was it to be his as well?

The light shimmered so brightly that Kira had to close her eyes, and even then she felt the burn behind her retinas. "I'm curious as to why such filth is interested in the human?"

The voice grew louder and Kira stumbled as she moved backward, deeper into the closet. Logan's tail slapped at her shoulders. She had no choice.

"Who sent you here? Who protects this human?" The voice was louder now, angry.

Heat seared her backside as a cloud of intense pressure tugged at her clothes. Kira yelped and almost fell to her knees, but she grabbed onto Logan instead, her fists sinking deep into the fur at his haunches.

Mist moved ever faster, gray swirls of cool, icy fog that coated both her and Logan in a cloud of energy. For a blessed moment the intensity of the mysterious stranger's light was gone and they were sucked toward the back of the closet. A roaring filled her ears and the pressure inside her head ramped up big time. It felt as if she were in the middle of a powerful vortex, one that if allowed, would rip her into pieces.

Kira had never felt so insanely alive and so very, very frightened. It was a weird dichotomy that left her full of adrenaline. The cells in her body felt as if they'd been seared from the inside out, and she clenched her teeth, pulling herself up onto Logan's back as the pressure behind them built.

All hell broke loose as Logan snapped his great jaw, taking off the hand of one of the trojans that had managed to get close enough to them. Dark liquid spewed everywhere, and the pain of it as it splashed onto her cheek ripped a scream from her throat.

It drove the point home. This was real. This was happening.

And these might be the last seconds of her life.

Kira's arms grabbed hold of Logan's neck as she positioned herself atop him, and she buried her head in his thick fur. He smelled of animal and anger and violence and protection. She closed her eyes and whispered, so softly she knew no one would hear.

"Just so you know—it was absolutely worth it."

The sound and chaos magnified, and Kira closed her eyes as tightly as she could and held on with the last bit of strength that she had. Every part of her screamed in pain, and she cried out, afraid and sad.

She was dying and there was nothing to do but meet her fate head on. The rush in her ears was near deafening, and it felt as if her head was going to explode.

Kira forced her eyes open—if she was to meet her end, she would see it coming. But the light was blinding and though she tried, she couldn't see anything. There was only the touch and feel of the animal she clung to. His warmth seeped into her bones, and for a second the sensation of floating drifted over her bones.

The pain disappeared. She sighed. And then there was nothing.

SILENCE SURROUNDED HER. Nothing but white noise in her ears. No screams from down the hall—Maggie-Mae freaking out because it was time for her meds; or Hank, the deaf giant, protesting his food choices. There were no messages over the intercom or the sound of shuffling feet.

No heavy breathing in her ear, or cold, clammy hands on her skin. There was nothing.

She liked it that way. Adrift on a sea of ignorance where a blanket of nothing meant the monsters in her head, the ones who populated her dreams, were slayed— however temporary.

Of course it couldn't stay this way—not in the world she inhabited. Slowly Kira became aware of a sound, like a plane drifting across a robin-egg blue sky on a hot summer afternoon. It droned a sad lament that was more of a nuisance at first, like a bee buzzing around her head, and then it pressed down on her. Hard.

She tried to inhale but realized she wasn't breathing. Had she ever been?

Her arms flailed and she tried to open her eyes as the

pressure in her chest mounted. As terror punched her square in the gut. She felt as if she was underwater. Everything was distorted. Everything *hurt*.

Where the hell was she?

Suddenly her lungs expanded and she inhaled great gulps of air. Her rib cage ached as if bones were broken, and it was cold, so very cold. Kira shuddered as she tried to understand all the sensations that slipped over her body and burrowed beneath her skin.

Images fell into her brain. A beast. Red eyes. Mergerone. Hands. Fists. Pain. And then him . . . the savior.

Logan.

The droning in her ear exploded, and she screamed as the pain inside became too much to bear. Her eyes flew open and she clawed at whatever it was that covered her—a blanket or something of the like. It was harsh and heavy and she kicked her legs as she wrestled with the shit-beige covering.

Whatever she lay upon moved as she rocked back and forth, and with a groan she shoved aside the covering, only to fall over the edge flat on her face. Nose against cold, hard tile. Every bone in her body ached, and it took a bit for Kira to steady her shaking nerves.

For several moments she stared down at the puffs of mist that fell from her nose. They reminded her of a cartoon she'd seen as a child. The one with the bull, scraping its hooves against the ground as it readied to charge. She raised her head and winced as the sounds that had been in the background erupted and filled the air around her.

It sounded like a bloody war was going on and she

was caught in the middle of it. Kira counted to three and then pushed herself to her knees. A growl sounded, the proximity of it suggesting whatever it was was close by. Was it Logan?

She stared down at the scars on her wrists, at the pale skin untouched by the sun for years. She rested back on her haunches and ran her hand through the short hair that barely touched her shoulders. It felt dirty, less than ordinary.

She was back. And unless this was some cruel illusion, she was alive.

Carefully Kira got to her feet and pushed the gurney out of her way as she stumbled forward. Overhead, fluorescent lights flickered, casting a surreal shadow over the carnage beyond. Blood, guts, and pieces of the creatures from the gray realm were scattered everywhere. It looked like a bucket of crimson had exploded over the walls and pristine tiles of what she now knew was the morgue at the Institute.

In the middle of all of it stood a tall man, his face in shadow, yet the dim recesses of his eyes glowed crimson.

Logan.

He was naked, his powerful frame bathed in a fine sheen of sweat and blood that emphasized the cut of his abs, the taut belly, and—her eyes lowered—everything else.

Kira had never seen anything so terrifyingly magnificent.

Logan nodded toward the mess on the floor. "Two of them made it through the portal."

She swallowed, not knowing what to say. Her mind was a mess of images, colors, and thoughts she didn't understand.

And God, she was so cold.

"We have to go. There's no time." He stepped into the light and she shivered at the savagery that clung to him. "I managed to close the portal behind us, but their master will be close on our heels. That bastard isn't governed by the same rules as the rest of us."

"I . . ." She shook her head, confused . . . uncertain.

The red of his eyes faded, a wary look replacing the fierceness of moments before. "I know you're scared, Kira, but you have to trust me."

She glanced at the mess that surrounded her. "That's a lot to ask. I don't even know you."

"I will keep you safe." His eyes were intense, his expression fierce. "I swear on all that matters to me. No one will hurt you again."

They stared at each other for several moments, and inside Kira, something stirred. Something broke. Melted. She believed him.

The door crashed open behind Logan and he paused, hands fisted.

"What the hell?" It was Mergerone. His nasally whine echoed into the sterile air and even with her hellhound close at hand, the fear inside Kira erupted. She whimpered and took a step back.

Logan's brow arched and he smiled, a cruel bent to his mouth as he turned.

The doctor stood frozen in fear and confusion, his

pale, pinched features seeming larger than life as he stared at the floor. His white lab coat was pristine, with "Mergerone" sewed into the chest pocket, the scarlet letters in bold print. When he spied Kira he made a sound—half sob, half scream—and tried to grab hold of the door, but he slipped on the blood that spilled over the tiles and went down hard.

"You're dead!" The doctor screeched as he rolled on the floor.

Logan was on him in an instant, his large body pinning the smaller man to the floor as his hands went around the doctor's neck.

Mergerone struggled, but it was no use, and his cowardly begging rang out between sobs as he ceased to move. "Don't hurt me. Please don't hurt me."

Logan bent his head and whispered harshly. "Nothing would give me greater pleasure than to rip your head off and shove it up your fucking ass."

"Oh God! Please, I'll do anything you ask."

"There's a special place in hell for filth like you." Logan's fingers glowed as he dug his right hand deep into the man's neck. The scent of burning flesh wafted into the air. Mergerone's scream ended on a yelp as the pressure became too much and he struggled to breathe.

"I've no time to deal with you myself, but make no mistake." Logan pushed away and stood swiftly. The air around him blurred and for a second the beast shone through. Kira saw it reflected in Mergerone's wild eyes.

She loved that he was scared shitless.

A dark stain appeared between the man's legs and

when Mergerone mouthed *"please,"* Kira wanted to smash her hand into his face.

"That's my mark, you son of a bitch." Logan spat.

Kira saw a red and raw crescent-like burn on Mergerone's neck.

"Be warned," Logan continued. "One of my brothers will be back for you, and where you're going," he smiled savagely, "there will be no escape."

Logan turned and held his hand out toward Kira. She stared at it for several seconds. She knew she was on the precipice of another life-changing moment. Did she run from all of it or trust in Logan?

"Kira, we have to go."

His voice was rough, the timbre intimate, and yet she sensed his confusion as well. It was then that she realized every single moment of her life had led to this point. If she never saw Logan again, he would still walk beside her every second of every day.

How could he not? She'd lived and breathed his memory.

Kira took a step forward. She didn't want the memory. She wanted the real deal.

Logan moved suddenly, his arms grabbing her close, pulling her up against his chest. He ran from the morgue, his long legs carrying them past the front desk and out into the humid Florida evening. Kira melted into his warmth and her last coherent thought was of the cicadas.

About how their song had never sounded so sweet.

And of the man who held her.

Of how it felt as if he was the home she'd never had.

Chapter Thirteen

"SHE'S RESTING COMFORTABLY."

Logan glanced up and nodded at Bill. He settled his large frame into the too-small wooden chair as best he could and took a long draw from the cold beer in his hand. Shadows clung to the corner he'd chosen, and though he appeared relaxed, he was, in fact, wound tighter than a tornado about to touch ground.

He'd met Bill at a large hotel somewhere along the border between Texas and Mexico. The Texan—not the most original of names. Bill had assured Logan the rambling bordello-style place was a safe haven, but still, he was wary.

Logan's dark eyes scanned the entire room and he shifted, trying to alleviate the tight muscles that stretched across his shoulders. God, he was tired. He'd driven like a bat out of hell to get to Texas after deciding he couldn't chance a normal shift. Logan wasn't sure that

Kira's already weakened body could take another trip through space and time. He'd stolen an SUV—pointed it northeast—and had laughed like hell when he'd realized it belonged to Mergerone.

A satisfied grin stole over Logan's face. Mergerone, the slimy fucker, would meet an end worthy of the filthiest of scumbags.

His thoughts drifted to the woman upstairs. She'd not woken the entire time it had taken them to get to the border and he was more than a little worried. Was there permanent damage?

"Is Kira going to be all right?" he asked, surprised to realize just how anxious he was to know her status.

Bill grabbed the seat across from him and grinned, the round jowls of his cheeks jiggling slightly as he settled himself in the wooden chair. "Oh yes. In a few days she'll be good as new. I've seen to it."

Logan's fingers tightened around the beer bottle as he stared at the Seraphim. Bill had at least dialed down the glam factor since his last visit, and was wearing plain denim jeans and a jacket that, while not unfashionable, did not sport pink, shiny lapels.

A shout drew Logan's attention and he glanced over at a group of men hanging near the bar. The room was full, though as far as he could tell the only otherworld creatures in the entire place sat at his table.

Logan took another swig of his beer and then set the empty bottle on the table. He got to his feet. "I'm glad she's going to be all right."

"Better than new, as I'm sure you'll be glad to know."
Bill grinned up at him, his smile lopsided, his full cheeks
flushed red. His eyes shimmered and Logan bristled at
the display of power that resided in their depths.

He took a step back and nodded. "That's great, but
you've got me confused with someone who gives a shit."
He sounded like a cold bastard, and the table jiggled
slightly as Bill's eyes narrowed. Good. The little turd was
finally getting it. Logan Winters didn't give a flying fuck
about Bill's agenda. About the fucking League of Guardians. He'd done his part. As for Kira, well, he could admit
that he was relieved she'd made it through the shift back
and that it appeared she'd be okay. He might even have
entertained the idea of Kira and . . . himself? Was he nuts?

He scowled and cursed. Best to let it rest.

"I think it's time for me to leave. I don't belong topside." Logan said flatly.

"You will stay." Bill rose and even though the top of
his head barely reached Logan's chest, there was no mistaking the power that existed inside his small form. Logan's empty beer bottle rattled and jerked its way toward
the edge until it teetered precariously, less than an inch
from falling. "I fear the tide is changing. The peace we've
enjoyed for so long is about to end."

"Seriously, Bill, you sound like a goddamn politician."

Bill ignored his sarcastic comment. "An ill wind rides
the horizon and the League needs to stand firm."

Here it was. Crunch time. Logan decided he'd play
along—at least until he was able to dig out the truth.

He leveled a steady gaze on Bill. "The bastard after Kira is one of your own. He stank to high heaven of the upper realm." Logan snorted. "No offense."

Bill's eyebrows rose, their thick wiry strands almost comical as the little man stared up at Logan. "You're sure of this." It wasn't a question so much as a statement, and judging by the expression on Bill's face, it was obvious the little shit wasn't surprised.

Logan nodded. "He's definitely shooting golden glow out of his ass; I just don't know *how much*."

Bill's face tightened. "I need you to stay with the girl. I can't chance her safety with anyone else—"

"No fucking way." Logan exploded, his voice carrying loudly and drawing the attention of most of the room. He bent closer. "I told you I was out. The only reason I did this was because of my mother. I held up my end of the bargain and I expect you to do the same."

The Seraphim stared up at him for several long moments. Bill finally answered. "I will not reveal your mother's identity but you cannot leave."

Logan turned around. "Watch me."

"Kira will perish without you."

The words whispered inside his head and Logan froze, his large frame thrumming with anger. What game was this?

"What the hell does that mean?" Images of Kira sank into his brain. Full of sun and golden skin, intermingled with the battered, dead body he'd first encountered.

The taste of her was still in his mouth and the feel of her was on his skin. There was a connection there—

something he really didn't want to think about. What was the point? She was human. He was a hellhound. Besides, she'd been marked by both the underworld and the upper realm. Complication was her new middle name.

Complicated was something Logan Winters wanted to avoid.

"If she dies all will be lost. You've tasted her soul, Logan. You followed her into the gray realm and you brought her back when there was no one else. Can you really leave Kira to the mercy of those who would end her?"

Logan stepped back, not liking where the conversation was going. The corners of the room were closing in and he tugged at the collar of his jacket. Christ but it was hot.

"Why the hell can't you look after her?" he snarled.

Bill's mouth thinned. "You know I cannot directly involve myself in the affairs of humans. That is not negotiable. Especially ones that hold the interest of the otherworld. It would risk exposing the very group of people who can help her. I can't be with Kira all the time and she needs to be guarded 24/7."

"I'm a hellhound . . . I don't do topside and I sure as fuck don't think that little slip of a human can survive below."

"There are ways."

"No."

"You're being stubborn."

"You're being a dick. I told you I was out."

"You care for her. I see it in your eyes."

"I hardly know her."

"Her future is linked to yours."

"Listen, Askelon," Bill's words sunk in and Logan faltered. A few seconds of silence passed and then he said softly, dangerously, "What did you say?"

Bill ran pudgy fingers across his shiny bald head. He sat down once more and motioned for Logan to do the same.

Logan exhaled harshly, aware that they were garnering just a little bit more attention than he liked. He slid into the chair and glared at Bill. "Tell me." He said tersely.

"I don't know the exact details—"

"Your kind never does," he interrupted. "You pull your puppet strings and move your chess pieces with one hand while doling out the barest of information with the other." Logan bent forward, his eyes glowing red as his animal shifted beneath his skin. "I'm not playing anymore. You either tell me the whole truth or I walk."

Bill held his gaze for a long time and then nodded toward the chair, his face grave. "Sit." At Logan's growl he lowered his voice. "Please. I've a story to tell."

AN HOUR LATER Logan let himself into the room Bill had readied for Kira. The blinds were drawn and the light was dimmed. It was a simple room, with pale cream walls free of decoration, and sparse furnishings of sturdy oak. The red and black threadbare carpet had seen better days, and Logan chose to ignore the stains, some of which appeared to be blood.

The bed was a four-poster, a wrought iron contraption that was dated, most likely an antique from two hundred years ago. And that pretty much summed up his impression of this backwoods town.

Modern conveniences seemed to have passed the place by.

His gaze settled onto the bed and he froze, surprised that Kira was awake and sitting up. Her back was to him and he was struck at how frail she looked with her shoulders hunched over and pale arms held tight to her body. The seam of her spine was visible through the cotton shirt she wore.

He clenched his hands at the sight. How he wished he could finish Mergerone. Drag his sorry ass to hell and dole out the heaviest of sentences upon him. Logan smiled at the thought and made a mental note to talk to his brother, Lucian, personally.

Kira turned her head to the side and for a moment an uncomfortable silence fell between them. He thought of everything that Bill had told him and acknowledged the truth. She was his. From the moment he'd tasted her soul, she'd belonged to him. He'd marked her as surely as she'd claimed him.

There was no going back. There was only the consummation.

She cleared her throat and whispered hoarsely, "You're still here."

"Yes."

"I thought you'd be gone by now."

"You sick of me already, Dove?"

She was shivering, and he moved closer but stopped at her panicked plea. "No, I don't . . . please don't look at me."

Logan swore under his breath as he took the remaining steps until he was in front of her, staring down at her bleached head, with inch long black roots. She still wore her faded green clothes from the Institute and he scowled when he caught sight of the blood splatter that decorated her shirt.

"You need to get out of those clothes."

Congealed blood marred her skin, but thanks to Bill's ministrations the bruising along her arms and neck was fading. But she was filthy. Who wouldn't be? The girl had been beaten to death.

Her entire body trembled and she locked her feet together in an effort to control it, while sliding her hands beneath her thin legs.

"I need a lot of things, but mostly I just need you to leave."

"Less than twenty-four hours ago you were singing a different tune."

"Twenty-four hours ago doesn't matter anymore." She turned her hand over and he caught sight of the scars on her skin. "Nothing matters. Nothing's changed."

"Everything has changed." He bent down in front of her. She had no clue. "And I already told you. I'm not going anywhere."

She exhaled slowly, but kept her head lowered. "Why?"

Because you'll be hunted and without me you will die. Because apparently your future is tied to mine. Because the only way to make sure you survive is for me to. . .

"Bill asked me to." He answered instead.

"Bill?"

"The short, round shit who saved you."

A violent shudder racked her frame and this time she did look up. Her dark eyes were shadowed with pain, fear, and confusion. Her gaunt cheeks were sunken, her lips colorless, and the cut above her mouth—though on the mend—looked raw against her pale flesh.

"I thought *you* saved me."

"No." He knelt down so that their eyes were level with each other. She would have looked away but he grabbed her chin and held her still. He needed to do this right. Needed to make her understand. "To be honest, you saved yourself, because you were brave enough to listen and react in a situation where most humans would freak the fuck out." He couldn't help himself and slid his hand along her delicate jaw. Damn but she was cold. Her eyes hung like luminescent jewels and in that moment Logan thought that he could stare into them for hours.

Kira tried to move her head but his grip was too strong, so she closed her eyes instead and whispered, "Don't look at me." A single solitary tear wove its way down from the corner of her eye and Logan dried it with a gentle swipe of his mouth. Christ, a week ago, "gentle" and Logan Winters were not something most people would put together.

He didn't do "gentle." He was as hard-assed as they came, but for her he'd damn well try.

"Open your eyes," he commanded. She kept them squeezed tight. "Kira, open your eyes." Logan threw in a dose of compulsion, and wariness looked back at him as she did his bidding. The harsh color of her bleached hair only served to emphasize how pale she was. "Why don't you want me to look at you?"

"I don't look anything like . . . like what I did back there." She paused. "Back in the gray realm. There I was perfect, but here," she shook her head, "here, I'm broken. A ghost of what I was . . . of what I want to be." She laughed bitterly. "How ironic is that? The only way I can be the person I want to be is if I'm dead."

She fingered the damaged skin at her wrist and he drew her hand into his. "We all have scars, Kira. Some are visible, but the most painful ones are hidden. Don't be embarrassed to show your weakness. You're alive and that kind of strength trumps the shit out of whatever this represents." His fingers traced the scars at her wrist and she shuddered violently beneath his touch.

She opened her mouth to say something but then closed it.

"I'm not crazy about the blond hair, but hey," he grinned at her, "we can fix that, right?"

Her bottom lip trembled—he felt her weakening— and without pause, Logan scooped Kira into his arms, holding her close to his chest as he kicked open the door to the bathroom.

"Logan, please put me down." Her words ended on a sob and something broke inside of him at the sound.

His arms tightened and he dropped his head, inhaling the scent of her—the one that was still full of sunlight and honey and something else. Something he'd not experienced in centuries. *Promise.* He used his booted toe to start the water running in the bath.

"What are you doing?" She whispered.

Logan stared down into her eyes. Bill had told him a lot of shit he'd not wanted to hear. Stuff about duty and the League. About fate and consequence. He'd made it clear that Kira needed to survive, and that Logan was the key.

Holding her felt like all kinds of right, and for the first time in hundreds of years Logan knew he was where he was supposed to be. He had no idea where this road was going to take him. Didn't even care about Bill's so-called prophecy. He tried not to think about the child that would figure into all of this. Kira's child. His child.

Instead he nuzzled her neck. Inhaled her scent and took it deep into his lungs. He would do the only thing he could to save her. He would claim her as his own and kill anyone who would dare to take her from him.

"Logan?" Her voice was soft, hesitant.

He drew in a ragged breath. "I'm going to do my damnedest to make your ghosts disappear."

Chapter Fourteen

KIRA SHIVERED EVEN as the room filled with hot steam from the bath. She closed her eyes and rested her head on Logan. Beneath her fingers his heart beat heavy against his chest. It vibrated, singing a song that held her entranced—a melody that for a time chased all her demons away.

He was strength and security. A lifeline to hope and promise. She should be scared as hell, and yet . . . she wasn't. In his arms there was some kind of contentment, which was so strange, considering she barely knew him.

I've known him for fifteen years. The words whispered through her mind and she knew them as the truth. Logan Winters had been a silent companion to her for all those years at the Institute. She'd found strength in his memory—in the very idea of him. He'd rescued her when she was ten and she supposed she'd always thought he'd come for her again.

And he had.

For years she'd felt as if she were living in slow motion. As if the days and weeks and months had blurred into one long string of abuse, confusion, and fear. And yet in the space of a few hours her world had tilted off center and settled into a place she'd never expected.

It was a world where the savior and the beast were one in the same. A world where the monsters from her nightmares were real. A world where the things that hadn't yet come to pass were very much a possibility.

And the child. The small boy with fiery eyes and dark curls. Where did he figure in all of this?

"I'm so tired," she said softly.

Logan's hands slid up her arms until they settled upon her shoulders. His breath was warm against her neck and the timbre of his voice vibrated inside her. She shivered once more as he spoke. "The water's ready."

Carefully he set her onto her feet and though Kira tried to be strong, she swayed and grabbed at his chest, her fingers fisting into his t-shirt.

"I've got you." He murmured.

Kira's eyes remained closed as his hands traveled down her back until he grabbed the edge of her shirt and slowly pulled it upward. She held her arms aloft and when cool air drifted across bare flesh, she quickly covered herself. Ashamed. Frightened. Anxious.

She felt his hands at her waist.

Bit her lips at the gentle tug on her waistband and tried like hell to remain still as he pulled her pants down to her ankles. Still, with eyes closed, she stepped out of her clothes and turned from him.

Logan's hands were on her hips—fire burned in their wake, and she jerked, her knees buckling beneath her. He was there and scooped her back into his arms and then he set her into the tub full of hot water. It slid over her tired, aching limbs and for a second she tensed, but as the heat absorbed into her flesh, Kira eventually relaxed.

Hands soon joined the water that lapped at her body. Fingers smoothed her skin with soap, slid over her stomach and up her rib cage and to her breasts, where they lingered—but only for a moment. Her nipples were already hard pebbles and they ached as he glided over them, spreading electric heat along the way.

He worked his magic up to her shoulders and to the back of her neck. Heat from his mouth blew over her flesh there, spreading goose bumps across her skin and awakening such longing that it was painful.

And still she kept her eyes closed.

"Sit up a bit." His words sounded forced, and Kira moved at his urging, her hands bracing either side of the tub as he wove his magic down her back—kneading her sore muscles until all the knots disappeared.

Logan pushed her back and then tugged a leg forward, up and out of the water. His hands worked their way down her thigh, then to her knee until he gently scrubbed her foot. Then he did the same for the other, taking his time as he lathered up her ankle and massaged the arch. When he was done, she was a mass of electrified nerve endings that screamed for his touch and cried out at the loss.

Don't stop. The words echoed inside her head.

Kira's chest rose and fell in rapid, exaggerated breaths.

She'd never felt as alive as she did at this moment, nor as scared.

Her hands covered her breasts once more, and she sat up, knees locked together, suddenly unsure. What the hell was she doing? Cool air caressed her face and for a second she thought he'd left, but then Logan spoke, his voice rough and bordering on loss of control.

"Open your eyes." He was there, right beside her.

She exhaled slowly and licked her lips, more than a little confused.

Kira did as he asked and as her gaze settled upon Logan, everything inside her stilled. Her heart lurched and for a moment it was painful for her to breathe. Or maybe she wasn't breathing at all.

"What are we doing?" Was that her voice? Full of smoke and whisper?

His eyes morphed into deep crimson and as his nostrils flared, she sensed the beast that lived inside him, lurking beneath the surface. Instead of scaring her, the thought of such a wild creature only served to excite. To inflame.

The throb that had begun minutes earlier, there between her legs, erupted with a fury, and the accompanying ache drew a groan from her lips as she shifted in an effort to alleviate the tension.

"I think you know, Kira."

God, the way he said her name, with that slight accent on the "r," made her weak.

"But . . ." How could she articulate the questions—the notion that someone like him would want someone like her? Someone broken and damaged? She glanced at the scars upon her wrists. "But, why?"

His ice blue eyes glittered and the rumble she heard in his chest was powerful. She stared into his eyes until she couldn't take it anymore, and when she would have closed her own, Logan growled. "Because you are mine."

Her eyes widened at that, and he licked his lips as if she were a delectable piece of food he was going to taste. And taste. And taste again.

"What are we doing?" she asked again. Her mind was muddled, and she was both afraid and filled with anticipation for his answer.

A wicked grin spread across Logan's face as he shed the last remnant of humanity. His jeans were thrown to the side and as he stood there—naked, powerful, and incredibly sexy—Kira knew she'd just taken a turn down a road from which there would be no return.

"Why, we're taking a bath, little Dove."

Her mouth went dry and she jerked backward. "But there's no—" She squealed as he slid into the tub, his large frame displacing a considerable amount of water.

"Room." She finished on a whisper.

"Yeah," he growled. "That's the point."

LOGAN'S HEART RAMMED against his chest and the beast that lurked beneath his skin stirred painfully. His cock was hard and he shifted in an effort to alleviate the discomfort.

The urge to mate—to mark her as his—was strong,

and he hissed, his teeth clamped together tightly, his jaw aching from tension. If it was anyone other than Kira with him now, he'd lose the fucking conscience, grab hold of the selfish bastard inside, and take her now.

She stared at him with those large exotic eyes full of fear, confusion, and yes, desire. He wanted to grab hold of her—press her naked breasts against him while he tasted the inside of her mouth. He wanted to part her legs and eat from the very center of her body. He wanted to lick and plunder and ease the ache in his cock.

He wanted Kira for himself with a need and an urgency that was unlike any other he'd ever felt. Suddenly things were clear in a way he'd never imagined. He'd wanted her all along. Even without Bill's whispered words. Without the League. In that moment he knew he'd never have left Kira.

He wanted her in every way imaginable and he would never let her go.

He would kill any who dared to take her from him. He would die for her.

Gone was the smile from his face. There was no way in hell he could keep up that façade. In its place was the hungry beast that existed inside his soul. The one that wanted to devour, to taste, and to touch. To control.

A low growl escaped him. The one that wanted to *claim*.

Her tongue darted out, a tasty pink treat that slid along her lips, leaving them soft and wet in its wake. His teeth glistened in the gloom as he slid forward and reached for her.

Kira didn't resist. She opened her mouth—to speak? He didn't know and he didn't care. Logan's right hand sank into the back of her head as he urged her forward and he took her mouth with a ferocious intensity that shocked him.

As his mouth opened and his tongue thrust inside her warmth, the primal nature that was the very heart of him cried out. *Mine.* He felt it in every fiber of his being.

Kira groaned beneath his onslaught and he moved her, bringing her between his legs, settling Kira's around his waist as the warm water lapped at their sides and slid over skin that was heated.

"Mine," he said fiercely against her mouth. The taste of her was exquisite. Honey and sunshine. Softness and passion—it filled every pore in her body. When he pulled away and gazed at her pale body against his dark skin, he saw through the veil, through that thin grasp of this human reality, and he reveled in the golden warmth of her spirit and soul as it glided over his flesh.

Her eyes widened as she followed his gaze. "Oh," she breathed.

His eyes flattened to a lead gray color. "Can you see that?" His voice rough and harsh, barely got the words out.

Kira nodded and ran her fingers along his forearm, and then crept up his chest. His hands slid down her back to settle on her butt and he pulled her against his straining cock as his mouth claimed the turgid nipple that dangled in front of him like a plump cherry.

She arched her back and whimpered as he kneaded

and sucked and used his tongue to taste. With one nipple already claimed, he held her in place, his free hand sliding downward. He paused—feeling her tense as he slowly sank his fingers between them—and the moan that escaped when he brushed against her clitoris nearly drove him insane.

"Mine," he whispered again as he broke free of her breast and pulled her mouth into his once more. She matched his passion with an intensity that should have surprised him, but didn't. Kira Dove may have been human but there was nothing ordinary about her.

"Logan, I've never—"

His fingers sank deep within her and she swore, "Oh, God," squirming against him, her hands and mouth searching, desperately trying to alleviate the need he sensed.

When a searching hand found his cock and gripped it along the head, he stopped. Fuck, he needed to get a grip or he was gonna blow early.

"Hold it. We gotta slow down." He whispered against her mouth.

"I can't." Kira stared down at him, her mouth bruised from his, her pale cheeks now flush with passion that he owned. Passion that he felt and shared. "I feel like I'm coming apart." She ground herself against him, her hand massaging the long length of his cock with a reckless abandon that made him harder than he already was.

He shifted and brought her head close. He inhaled her arousal. She was all around him. Inside him. He saw his feral need reflected in the glittering pools of her eyes.

"I've never wanted anyone before." She whispered hoarsely. He saw the pain and growled in anger, but her fingers across his lips silenced him. She shuddered and moaned. "Mergerone took my innocence and for a while my grip on reality." She was panting now, small animalistic sounds falling between her words as she continued. "But he never got close to the part of me that's alive right now." His fingers moved inside her, slowly and methodically, as she widened her legs and began to writhe. "The part of me that you awakened." She exhaled. "The part of me that belongs to you."

Logan snarled at her words, inflamed with passion and the need to claim. He gripped her head hard as the beast shifted beneath his skin. In her hands his cock swelled even more and he barely got the words out, so hard did he have to concentrate on keeping control.

"From this moment on you are mine." His eyes glowed crimson and the savagery of his animal flickered within their depths. "I will not touch another from this day forward. Do you understand what that means?"

She opened her mouth but no words were spoken. He knew she didn't fully understand what was about to happen. He grabbed her mouth once more and this time his tongue slid into her with a gentleness that made her moan and melt against his chest. *She will.*

He kissed her with a yearning matched by the need he sensed in Kira. Carefully he pulled her upward, into his arms, and he stepped out of the tub. He placed her against the countertop so that her back was to him and he held her in place, careful of her trembling legs.

Kira Dove might have been innocent in a lot of ways, but you'd never fucking know it by the way she tilted her butt and spread her legs. Logan growled harshly, and moved behind her, his crimson eyes claiming hers in the mirror that was on the wall.

Her breasts hung, swaying softly and swollen with need. Her mouth was open and her eyes were alive with passion. A small sound emerged from her throat—a cross between a whimper and a moan—and that's all it took.

"Don't take your eyes off mine," he ordered as his hands traveled down her back to rest at the base of her spine. He pushed her forward slightly and howled as he slid his long length deep inside her body.

One smooth, sure stroke.

Warmth and tightness surrounded him, and Logan paused for a moment, sweat breaking out along his body as he fought for control. Her mouth was open as she gasped, and his fingers dug into her shoulders. "Open your fucking eyes."

Her chocolate eyes flew open and he began to move slowly. In and out. Long, drawn-out thrusts that took him to the edge of control and made Kira whimper over and over, "oh my God, oh my God."

It gave Logan immense pleasure to hear her cry out as he increased the tempo, and when his fingers crept around and claimed her clitoris she screamed, her arms bracing themselves against the countertop.

Their eyes locked together as he slammed into her, and though Logan would have preferred to take things slower, to worship her in the manner that she deserved, he knew he couldn't do it. He was too close to the edge.

The walls of her vagina closed around him, tightly, and she clenched as her whimpers increased. He grimaced as his canines erupted and still her dark eyes watched. She was unafraid. Fearless.

He held her so tight that he knew she'd be bruised in the morning, but there was no going back. When he felt the pressure build—when his body strained and pumped and gripped—he roared and clamped on to her shoulder, biting down hard as the index finger of his right hand burned into her neck.

"Logan!" She screamed his name and he held on as she shuddered against him and climaxed. Still their eyes held. His body emptied into hers and he claimed her in the way of his people. He'd tasted her blood, fed from her soul, and marked her as his.

After several long moments, Logan felt her shudder and go limp in his embrace. He staggered backward and pulled her into his arms, kissing her forehead as he did so.

You're mine, Kira Dove. I'll kill anyone who would touch you.

Chapter Fifteen

IT WAS DAYLIGHT. The sun found its way through the thin slats of the cheap plastic blinds, and Kira gazed upon Logan's face. He was asleep, his features softened, younger-looking. Thick coffee-colored hair crept over his eyebrows, and his shadowed beard could give any Hollywood hottie a run for his money.

He slept on his back, one arm flung above this head, the other still across her waist. Even in sleep his possession was absolute.

Kira moved her legs and stifled a groan. After they'd made it to the bed, Logan had proceeded to make love to her for hours. His mouth and tongue, his fingers and cock had given her more pleasure than she thought possible. The things they'd done . . . the things he'd whispered, of pleasures yet to be experienced.

She was sore and blushed at the thought of the tenderness between her thighs. Of the throb at her shoulder where Logan had bit her. She cracked her neck and hissed at the stab of pain there—the one that said she belonged to someone.

Kira Dove had been adrift for years and she'd found harbor in the arms of the beast.

"Are you all right?"

Startled, she glanced up and inhaled sharply as his handsome face came into focus. "I am." Her brow furled and though she hated the dark thoughts that that lingered, she knew she needed to face them. "So, where do we go from here? I'm on someone's hit list and I'm assuming my name is still at the top."

His eyes darkened and he rolled over so that his head was level to hers. His hands crept along her jaw and he held her tenderly, though she sensed the anger that rode beneath his skin.

"No one will ever touch you again. Understand?" He bared his teeth and growled. "No one."

Kira nodded, but in truth she didn't really understand. There was so much she didn't know.

"Last night you said that," she paused and exhaled. "You said that someone named Bill saved me." She bit her lip. "I was beaten to death, Logan." She held her wrists up. "And save for these scars, there's nothing wrong with me. Hell, the whole gray realm thing is hard enough to fathom, but being dead and then brought back . . ."

Her voice trailed into silence and she let him pull her close. She rested her cheek against his chest, listened to him breathe. Her fingers splayed across him. He was real and she would focus on that.

"Bill is an ancient, powerful creature." His voice rumbled beneath her and Kira closed her eyes, content to just listen to him. "He's the one who ordered me to bring you back from the darkness when you were a child. He's also the one who sent me into the gray realm."

"Why?"

Logan paused, not really sure what or how much to tell her. "There are forces in this realm and beyond who would like to see your life ended. They fear what you represent."

God, Kira was so confused. "And what's that, exactly?"

"Hope." He said simply.

"Hope." She angled her head so that she could look into his eyes. They glittered in that intense way that made her catch her breath, and she felt a stirring hardness at her hip.

His hand slid to her lips. "You are the light that will keep the darkness at bay."

"The light." She repeated. Okay. "And the child?" The little boy with curls and eyes that looked so much like Logan. Pain lanced across her chest at the thought of him, and her hand fell back, drifting below to cradle her belly. Had they made a child last night? Was it *her* little boy she'd seen in her dreams?

"They would see him never born."

Kira was silent. She didn't know what to say to that.

Logan rolled her up onto his stomach and held her gently above him. "I will do whatever it takes to keep you safe, and the League is sworn to hold that vow as well."

"The League?" she asked softly, though in truth she was more focused on her sensitive nipples as they scraped along the rough hair that sprinkled across Logan's chest. It was an exquisite torture that filled her insides with an all-too-familiar heat.

"A group of warriors who've pledged allegiance to Askelon—or Bill, as he wants to be called."

"Oh." His eyes were now crimson and his cock was poised between her legs.

"I'll explain fully later." A wicked smile crossed his face. "Unless you want the details now?"

Kira groaned and bent her head to claim his mouth. She kissed him long and hard, lips sliding and tongue probing. When she came up for air, she muttered hoarsely. "The details can wait."

It was nearly dusk when Logan walked down to the common room at The Texan. The gentle swell of voices, the scent of greasy food and stale beer greeted him as he moved into the shadows.

Bill was there. He sensed him.

Logan strode toward the far corner, the one lodged between the ladies' room and the kitchen. He felt the unmistakable pop of a protection ward as he stepped in front of Askelon.

For a few moments there was nothing but silence. Bill's dress was muted, his small, round body covered in dull brown from the collar of his shirt with the rhinestone buttons to the tips of his worn boots. It didn't complement his ruddy complexion but it certainly went with the somber look in his eyes.

"She is yours."

Logan eyed him and nodded.

Bill cracked a smile, but it was one that remained near his mouth, never reaching the shimmering depths of his eyes. "Good. She belongs with you. I knew this." Bill looked away, his small hands clenched. "They will search for her." He glanced back toward Logan. "They won't stop."

"I'm taking Kira to my mother's," Logan answered quietly.

Bill looked surprised. "This is good. Until I know who hunts Kira Dove, I won't be able to keep her safe."

"No one will touch her while she's there, and I can fulfill my duties to the underworld without drawing attention to myself. The Overlord will never know . . . my father will never know, either."

Bill nodded, a smile breaking upon his face. "Yes, and she'll remain untraceable while with your mother. It's perfect."

Logan agreed. He turned and gazed out at the room full of humans, and for the first time sensed otherworld. Immediately his senses sharpened. His nostrils flared and he growled softly.

A vampire was in the corner opposite him and Bill. A female. His eyes narrowed and he penetrated the shadows that clung to her. Long auburn hair fell down past her chest and eyes of cerulean blue gazed toward the door. They held pain, want, and need. Her fangs were distended, her hands clenched at her denim-clad sides.

He turned and spied a tall dark-haired man who'd just walked into the place. The scent of magick clung to him. At his side was a blond woman, her arms around his waist as if he belonged to her. A shifter—jaguar, by the smell of him—said something to the sorcerer and headed for the bar.

Logan's gaze swung back to the vampire, but she was gone, and he realized that Bill was intensely focused on the drama, his strange eyes lingering on the now-empty corner.

"Who the hell is she?"

"Ana is a new protégé." Bill nodded toward her. "I'm very happy to see she's just passed an important test. The sorcerer O'Hara is someone who means a lot to her and I wasn't sure she'd be able to remain hidden with him so close."

"What would you have done if she'd revealed herself?"

Bill's eyes narrowed and winter coated his words. "It's good that she remained hidden." Bill glanced up at Logan, his eyes hard, unreadable. "The tide is turning and the League needs as many soldiers as we can get, by whatever means we deem necessary."

Bill drifted from sight but his voice lingered long after, echoing inside Logan's head.

"Don't ever doubt the lengths that I will go, to ensure our needs are met."

Logan blinked and felt a small, soft hand slip inside his. He glanced down at Kira and smiled, feeling his body relax almost immediately. Her blond mess of a head was growing on him.

"Who was that?"

"Bill."

"Oh." Her eyes widened. "He's gone? I would have liked to have met him." She blushed. "Well, at least, conscious this time."

Logan turned and locked his eyes onto the sorcerer. The man's smile faded and Logan sensed the power he held from across the room. "It's time to go, little Dove."

Logan and Kira hopped into the stolen SUV and pointed it north. As the Mexican sun reflected into the rearview mirror, Logan looked ahead. He thought of the one who was out there. The one who wouldn't stop until he had Kira. His hands gripped the steering wheel hard and he accelerated, feeling the need to go as fast as the machine would allow.

"Where are we going?" Kira's soft voice drew him from his dark thoughts.

Logan replied without skipping a beat. "We're going home."

"Home." She repeated. "I like the sound of that." She smiled at him and his heart twisted. His body heated with the need to protect. The need to keep this woman safe. "Where is that, exactly?"

He flipped the radio on. "It's where the sun is endless and the snow is covered in a blanket of diamonds."

She sighed and slid over until her small body pressed tight to his. "Sounds like heaven."

Logan smiled but didn't answer. *Lady, you have no idea.* He increased his speed and hummed along to the strains of Mötley Crüe's *Shout at the Devil.* How appropriate.

Seconds later only his taillights broke through the dusk, and the clouds of dust that floated above the road rose several feet into the air.

Then there was nothing.

Keep reading for an excerpt from

Wicked Road to Hell,

the first full-length novel in
Juliana Stone's
League of Guardians series,
available May 2012
wherever books are sold.

Chapter One

DECLAN O'HARA STEPPED into the middle of the cross-roads, a lonely stretch of pavement on the outskirts of town. The moon was barely visible, yet a thin ribbon of light bled through, basking the low-lying fog in an eerie glow.

He glanced to his right as a series of subtle vibrations shot up his legs.

Company was coming.

His hands were loose at his sides and he cracked his neck in an effort to relieve some tension.

Declan smiled in anticipation. *It was about time.*

His eyes pierced the gloom. An image wavered and solidified not more than three feet from him and the smile vanished, leaving his expression blank. He studied the newcomer for a few moments, relishing the fear he sensed.

"You're late." Declan's voice was low, the tone conversational, yet the hard glint in his eyes told a different story.

His visitor, a slight imp of a man, took a step backward and shook his head. "I got away as soon as I could." His voice was thin and there was a nervous edge to it.

Declan paused, welcoming the whisper of magick that rippled over his skin. "Where is he?"

The newcomer swallowed thickly, his Adam's apple protruding in a rapid jerk. "He's no longer in Los Angeles."

At Declan's frown the man continued. "He now has a protector . . . a vampire."

"A protector?" *Interesting.* "That's all you got?"

The slight man nodded slowly.

Unbelievable. Declan swore under his breath and turned away. What a complete waste of time. For fuck sakes, he'd given up a bottle of merlot and a hot blonde for this? His irritation was surpassed only by his desire to get back to the lady and salvage at least part of his evening. He stepped away.

"What about payment?"

Declan paused, letting the energy inside him gather until his fingertips hummed with the heat of his power. He glanced back, eyebrows raised. "Payment? You didn't give me anything I don't already know. I wanted the location."

"But I warned you of the protector—"

He laughed, though he wasn't amused. "You think I need to be warned?" The ground beneath them trembled and danger swept in on the breeze. Declan was pissed. He had no time for this shit.

"There's talk . . ." The man licked his lips nervously. "There's talk that he's been taken to New Orleans."

"Fact or fiction?" Declan was fast losing patience. It didn't take much to trigger his dark side these days.

"I can't be certain."

Declan turned once more to face him, his face hard, his eyes cold.

"I risked a lot to come here, to meet with you. If they find out . . ." The small man's eyes glowed, a tinge of red burning through the gloom as he snarled in anger. "Samael will kill me."

Declan's surprise at the informer's words was kept hidden. Samael? If the demon lord was involved, the game had just changed big-time. Declan's fingers twitched, his nostrils flared as the energy in his hands sparked.

"What does Samael want with him?"

"I will give you no more." The informer widened his stance and hissed. "I want payment."

There it was . . . the trigger.

Declan cocked his head to the side and gave his power free rein. Mist swirled ever faster, hiding the darkness he unleashed. Wind whipped along the surface of the road, moaning as it enveloped the informant in a blanket of death. Seconds later Declan stepped over the still form that lay at his feet.

"Consider that payment rendered." He grabbed his cell phone and hit redial.

"You get the intel?" Nico's rough voice filled his ear. The shifter was a jaguar warrior and Declan's partner.

"I'm headed to Louisiana. I'll let you know what I find

when I get there. We don't have much time. Samael's involved now."

"Samael?" Nico sounded surprised. "That can't be good. Who the hell *is* this guy we're tracking? Do we have a name yet?"

Declan's eyes narrowed. "No name." He paused as an owl hooted in the distance. "Check out Los Angeles, see if you can pick up his trail or find a bread crumb that's bigger than a nibble."

The line went dead.

Guess he was heading to the Big Easy.

DECLAN ARRIVED IN New Orleans well past midnight the following evening. The moon was in hiding, the air was cool, and the energy in the city was powerful. Ancient magick lived here, fed not only by the great Mississippi River that slid by in silence, but by the souls of the dead who refused to leave.

It had been ages since he'd last been here. Another lifetime. He shook the melancholy that threatened and sought out the French Quarter. The Voodoo Lounge was located amongst a host of venues on Decatur Street.

Declan headed that way, his tall form sliding amongst the tourists with ease, his dark good looks drawing many a female eye. He ignored them all—even the busty brunette with the large doe eyes and plump, candy red lips.

There wasn't time for such frivolities when the world was going to shit.

Decatur was party central in the Big Easy, and the heat from the bodies in the streets and sidewalks created a blanket of mist that hovered inches above the crowd, as it mixed with the cooler air.

It was an eerie glow that somehow fit the chaotic undercurrent in the air. It was the chaotic undertone he was worried about. Something was off here in the land of crawdaddies and mint julep. He continued along Decatur until he spied the sign he'd been looking for.

It wasn't hard to miss, being a shade past puke green with a splash of orange and yellow. THE VOODOO LOUNGE. He smiled as he neared the club. He didn't remember it being so . . . gaudy.

There was a crowd gathered along the sidewalk, and by the looks of it, no one was getting inside. Typical night in the Quarter.

A mountain of flesh guarded the entrance; his bald head and heavy features were intimidating—as were the mess of tattoos that adorned his flesh. His shoulders were as wide as the door, the muscles bulging from beneath a tight t-shirt, and his legs were leather encased, his feet booted.

The dude was otherworld. It was in the energy that slithered along the man's frame, invisible to the human eye, yet vibrant to someone like the sorcerer.

The bouncer was a shifter, one of Ransome's clan, no doubt.

Declan nodded. "Nice evening."

The incredible hulk cocked his head to the side but remained silent.

"Ransome in tonight?"

"Depends"—the bouncer spit to the side—"on who's asking."

"An old friend." Declan flashed a smile that never reached his eyes. "Tell him O'Hara's in town."

The bouncer's eyes narrowed. He turned his head slightly, murmuring as he did so, obviously talking into a com device. Seconds later he stepped aside and Declan was allowed entrance.

The Voodoo Lounge had been in existence for as long as Ransome LaPierre's family had been in New Orleans, and that had been several generations. It was an eclectic bar filled with all sorts of otherworld and a mixture of human as well. They came together in a melting pot of bodies, music, and sex.

It was the kind of place that easily bred darkness. As Declan eyed the revelers he felt the potency of the energy surround him, and along with it, the familiar tug of want.

The dark side was a seductive bitch. He'd tasted her secrets. And though he was bound to the light, sometimes the lines blurred.

His gaze wandered the room as he slid through the crowd. It was hot, frenetic. He spied Ransome LaPierre immediately. It was hard not to. The alpha of the LaPierre pack was a handsome son of a bitch with a mess of hair the color of dark tobacco. The wolf was holding court in the far corner, surrounded by cheesy velvet sofas, jugs of beer, and—Declan grinned—lots of women.

The werewolf arched a brow and moved two women off his lap, a slow smile spreading across his features as Declan approached.

"You want one?" the wolf asked as Declan approached. He grinned and shoved a tipsy blonde Declan's way. "Or two?" He nodded toward the brunette and laughed, his N'awlins accent rolling off his tongue with devilish glee. "Bookends, no?"

Declan shook his head, though his eyes lingered on the generous rack that was nearly falling from the lady's too-small tank top. *Lady* being an extremely loose term.

"We need to talk." His tone was clipped.

Ransome's smile faded, and he stood in one fluid motion. The man was tall and had an inch or two on Declan, putting him near six-foot-six.

The blonde stepped in front of Declan, her hand falling to his chest. "What's the rush, sugar? Don't you wanna play?" She laughed softly. Her eyes were dilated, filled with the synthetic happiness of whatever kind of drug she'd ingested.

"Not interested." He removed her hand and followed Ransome, ignoring the expletives she shouted after him. The dense crowd parted like the Red Sea, allowing them easy access to Ransome's office located on the upper level of the bar.

The door closed behind them, muffling the heavy beat of the band. Declan exhaled slowly and watched as Ransome poured a generous tumbler of bourbon, but declined when the wolf offered him a glass as well.

Ransome smiled lazily, his slow Louisiana drawl falling from his lips like a melody. "So, what brings you back to these parts, my friend?"

"I'm looking for someone."

Ransome snorted. "Aren't we all?"

"This one's special."

Again the wolf laughed. "Aren't they all?"

Declan shook his head. "Not like this one."

The smile that graced the wolf's face fled immediately and his eyes narrowed. Declan nodded. Now he had his full attention.

Ransome took a long swig of bourbon, hissing as it went down, though his eyes never left Declan's.

"Where you been for the last two years?"

The wolf's question took him by surprise, and Declan was silent for several seconds. *To Hell and back.*

"Around," he answered softly as he eyed the shifter closely.

Ransome smiled though his eyes remained aloof. "It's a dangerous world, my friend, and we don't always know who the enemy is. A little elaboration would be welcome."

Declan didn't like where the conversation was headed. He had no time for posturing.

"It's common knowledge you broke ties with the Castille brothers, but the rumors of your whereabouts have been murky at best. You working alone?"

Declan wasn't surprised at Ransome's words. The werewolf had always kept a paw on the pulse of the otherworld. "No," he replied dryly. "I've got a new boss."

An image of Bill flashed in front of his eyes and he

clenched his teeth together tightly. The little bastard was one of the Seraphim, angelic creatures who had absolute dominion over the upper realm. They also dipped into the affairs of humanity or wherever else they saw fit.

Two years ago Bill had pulled Declan from the bowels of Hell. Unfortunately his one-way ride out of darkness had come with a price. The Seraphim currently owned Declan's ass for several lifetimes to come. He was now part of a group of soldiers known as the Seraph. They did the bidding of the Seraphim, no questions asked.

"A name would be good."

"I don't have time to play twenty questions, LaPierre."

The werewolf studied him in silence and a slow burn of frustration hit Declan's skin.

"What does your boss want with this *person* who's *different*?"

Declan's anger spiked and rode the edge of pissed-off. "My new deal doesn't come with a lot of answers. I do as I'm told and move on."

LaPierre poured himself another drink, this time not offering the same to Declan.

"Nothing is ever as it seems, O'Hara."

"No shit," he answered, his voice tight. "Bill might be an arrogant little prick but he's Seraphim."

Ransome's eyes narrowed at that. "And how's that going?"

Declan grabbed a decanter of whiskey off the wolf's shelf and poured himself a double. "Don't ask." He downed the contents in one gulp, welcoming the fire as the liquid burned its way down to his gut. "You hear any chatter on the street? Otherworlders new to the area that don't belong? Or has my trip here been wasted?"

"A trip to Decatur Street is never wasted, O'Hara."

"Normally I'd agree, but I've no time to play and even less time to find this bastard."

"I might know something." A lazy grin spread across Ransome's face, and yet his eyes were dead serious as he focused on Declan.

"Might?" Declan asked.

"I've got a couple of conditions."

Declan eyed his old friend closely. "And they'd be . . ."

"I don't want a holy war running amok in my backyard. Keep your boss out of my city."

No worries there. Bill was with Azaiel. He was one of the original Seraphim but had fallen from grace centuries ago, lured from the upper realm by a beautiful eagle shifter. *Dumb fuck.*

He'd created a portal that had almost ripped a hole the size of Hell into the human realm. A lot of people had suffered, given their lives in order for the portal to remain hidden. Declan's own father, Cormac, had tried to get his slimy hands on the damn thing.

Azaiel had languished in the Hell realm for eons, but two years ago he'd been retrieved and now was on trial for his sins.

As far as Declan was concerned, the fallen was going to get what he deserved. Bill would be busy for days.

Declan nodded. "Done, and the second?"

Ransome grabbed a coat from the chair behind his desk. "I'm coming along."

"Not possible." Declan shook his head. "I'm working this one alone."

Ransome ignored him and slipped supple leather over his powerful shoulders. "You forget, sorcerer, that this is my town, and nothing of significance happens without my knowledge or involvement."

Declan's lips thinned but he remained silent. He could use dark magick to stop him, Ransome had no idea the kind of power that lived beneath his skin, but he couldn't deny the wolf was one hell of a tracker.

He nodded and stepped aside, following Ransome out the back door. He'd humor the wolf for the moment.

Besides, Bill would fucking hate the idea.

About the Author

JULIANA STONE lives with her family and dog somewhere in Canada. Her passion for music and the written word has been a lifelong addiction, and in addition to writing, she ventures out occasionally to perform with her band mates. She loves all things paranormal, '80s rock, spending time with her family, and sports. Juliana is currently at work on her next book in the *League of Guardians* series.